THE
FRIENDSHIP
DIVIDE

A Friends-to-Lovers Romance

ANNE TROWBRIDGE

THE FRIENDSHIP DIVIDE

A
Friends-to-Lovers
Romance

ANNE TROWBRIDGE

Cruz Into Love Series: Book 2

ISBN: 979-8-9865072-6-2

For my sister, Marisa.

*You're independent, courageous, and always up for an adventure.
It makes sense to dedicate a book about siblings to you,
but you're more than a sister.*

*Thanks for being one of my best friends
and loudest cheerleaders, too.*

Other Books by Anne Trowbridge

Cruz Into Love Series

The Distance Between Us:
A Hidden-Identity Romance (Book 1)
(also available now in Kindle Vella)

The Friendship Divide:
A Friends-to-Lovers Romance (Book 2)
(also available now in Kindle Vella)

What Separates Us:
An Enemies-to-Lovers Romance (Book 3)
(coming soon, but available now in Kindle Vella)

The Curveball Incident Series

Curveball: A Love Story (Book 1)

Curveball: A Wedding Novella (Book 1.5)

Out of the Park: A Romance (Book 2)

Thrown: A Baseball Romance (Book 3)
(coming soon, but available now in Kindle Vella)

Sliding: Jim's Story (Book 4)
(coming soon, but available now in Kindle Vella)

Ticket to Love Series

The Honeymoon: A Second-Chance Romance (Book 1)
(also available now in Kindle Vella)

The Bridesmaid: A Romantic Suspense Story (Book 2)
(also available now in Kindle Vella)

Chapter 1

Family Obligations

"I'VE SEEN GERIATRICS with younger souls than yours," Tyrone said, his disapproving shake of the head at odds with the smirk that was beginning to tug on the corner of his mouth. "My grandma's got more game."

"Honestly, she probably does," I admitted. My reward for that particular honesty bomb was a snort of laughter from him, but I couldn't exactly be mad. I mean…he wasn't wrong. I was 28 years old on the outside and ready for retirement on the inside.

"Why do you even have those tattoos and muscles and pretty boy looks if you're not going to bother using them for good, my brother?" Tyrone went on, leaning against the door of the training room at the gym where we both worked. "I've got a whole crowd going out tonight, including some women who would be all over you. Join us. Jake, my man, for once in your life, let your inner wild animal loose."

"I appreciate the invite, I really do," I replied as regret bubbled up deep inside of me where, trust me, no inner wild animal existed. In a different life, in a different set of circumstances…maybe. Maybe I'd be crawling all over town every night with Tyrone and his group of friends, lighting it up with a drink in one hand and the other arm wrapped around some beautiful woman. But that had never been my life to lead, not even in high school or college. "But I've got family obligations tonight," I told him.

"Family obligations," he mimicked, his tone teasing but I saw the look of annoyance that fluttered across his face. Ty would give up on me altogether at some point, I knew, and then these invitations would stop. They were already getting more infrequent. After all, I'd never once said yes. "Tell me the truth, Jakey-boy, are you in the mafia? Or, wait, part of a motorcycle club?"

"Not those kinds of family obligations," I said with a chuckle. "Dinner."

"Okay, grandpa, whatever you say." He shook his head again. "Tell the other residents at your nursing home that I said hi."

I gave a half-hearted wave as he pushed off the door jamb and headed out. As he disappeared around the corner, I worked to smother the regret that was still trying to gain traction inside me. I knew I could make it disappear if I worked hard enough. I was a champion at shoving away my worries and disappointments, like a human trash compactor of emotions. Everyone has their special talent, and that one's mine.

Wearily I grabbed my things and headed out, too. I needed to get home and get ready for the family dinner. I hadn't been lying to Ty about it, and despite how he'd made me wish for carefree times, the dinner was a good thing. A celebration rather than an obligation.

But before any of that could happen, I needed to make my first stop of the evening at my parents' house to check on my mom. She would not be part of the dinner because she wasn't invited. My brothers and I are the family I've been talking about. My parents, on the other hand…well, they're obligations two and three on my long, soul-cracking list.

*   *   *

I parked my truck in their driveway and eyed the

front yard. The hedges under the bay window were a haphazard, overgrown mess, and the grass was starting to droop lazily, brought low under the burden of its own weight. Their yard work was also on my obligation list, but I clearly had it set at an even lower priority level. I grimaced at the weeds clawing through the sidewalk cracks as I made my way up the front steps.

"Mom!" I called, letting myself into the foyer. "It's Jake." I don't know why I bothered telling her that. I was literally the only person who would possibly be visiting this house.

"Hi, honey," she replied, walking out of the kitchen with a glass of heaven knows what in her hand. Her gait was already a little unsteady. "How was work today?"

"Fine." We had this almost-identical non-conversation regularly. I don't know what she'd do if I ever launched into actual details about my day at the gym. Or, for that matter, any aspect of the world of responsibility that she'd been cheerfully letting me shoulder since I was a kid. "Did you see dad today?"

She paused to take a sip from her glass before planting herself in the recliner. "No," came the terse reply. That recliner had always been dad's favorite spot, and he'd watched an infinite number of football games and other assorted sporting events there. She lost no time in taking it over once he vacated it. "You know how hard it is for me to get there."

"Want me to take you?" I offered, although I was pretty sure I knew what her answer would be. Going to see dad meant facing a whole lot of reality. Too much, in fact. Reality and Hazel Cruz had a falling out a long time ago, and she wasn't looking to mend those fences.

"Maybe," she murmured noncommittally. "Where

are your brothers? Aren't they with you?"

"No," I said with a roll of my eyes. Neither of my brothers had even driven by this house in years, and I thought she would have accepted their absence by now. They likely would never come here again, and they were both just fine with that. So she needed to be fine with it, too. "I just wanted to check in before I go home. You're good?"

"I'm fine, Jake. Just fine." Her eyes were on the television despite the sound being turned down so low that she almost certainly couldn't hear it.

"Okay, I'll head out then," I said, stopping to grab a stack of bills off the table. I'd been managing their finances for a while now.

"Thank you for stopping by," she replied, not bothering to look at me as I headed to the door. "But everything is just fine."

Right, I thought.

As irritation tried to break free of the emotional prison inside of me, I locked her front door and walked to my truck. I climbed in and leaned my head back, closing my eyes as I worked to shove that irritation further down. I didn't have time to be resentful or irritated. I'd spent a lot of years burying all my emotions deep inside of me, after all, and I couldn't afford to start letting any of them loose now.

Or ever.

Chapter 2

The Joke

IT WAS THE JOKE, I finally decided as I tossed back a gulp of whatever was in my glass. Still eyeing the happy couple, I set the glass, ice cubes clinking, back on the table with more of a thud than I'd intended. As the curious eyes of our group moved to me, I gave a shrug in apology. My jerky motions got a raised eyebrow from my amused brother, but soon they were all chatting again, my clumsiness forgotten.

Guess that meant I was doing a passable job of keeping my inner turmoil hidden. But then of course I was—it really *was* a special talent of mine. No one knew about the emotional prison inside me, not even my brother Max, who I loved more than anyone or anything in this world. I said my parents were priorities two and three on my list? Max was number one. Always had been.

So, yeah, I was a master at hiding things. Yet even I couldn't believe how this dinner was affecting me. I was rattled, and those hidden emotions were threatening to stage a riot.

I didn't want to be jealous of the happiness Max had found. And certainly I couldn't begrudge him this celebration of better times to come. No one deserved the happiness he'd found more than he did. I needed to tie that jealousy right back down. This was Max's night and it needed to stay that way.

I was working like mad to re-bury those thoughts

as I watched the other people at our table interact. There was Max, of course, who I'd basically devoted my entire life to since our father did his best to destroy him. Then there was his new girlfriend Lily, a human beam of sunshine who was currently laughing at something Max said, her blue eyes shining with love every time she locked gazes with him.

Seeing them together was so beautiful it almost hurt physically, like I'd gotten a sunburn from staying too close to all those rays of happiness. Lily's best friend Claire was the other member of the party. I kept catching her quietly analyzing the happy couple, a look of satisfaction on her face. It seemed like seeing Max and Lily together was hitting all her joy receptors, too. I mean, really, just being with them was so powerful that it *should* have been producing a contact high. Their love absolutely radiated from each small touch and intimate glance they shared.

I wanted to experience that kind of love for myself someday, and I guess that's partly what was stirring up my angst. The truth of the matter was that years ago I'd given up pursuing my own wants and desires to make sure Max could realize his. That's why the inner party animal Tyrone was searching for didn't exist. That's why I had a list of other family obligations a mile long. That's why I had to keep my dreams and feelings on lockdown. It was all for Max, and I'd do it the same way if given the chance. So I'm not saying I regret anything. But…well, sometimes the emotions got to rioting and had to be put back in their cells.

The thing that kept me in check was the thought that I'd be as bad as my dad if I begrudged Max even an ounce of joy. For years, Max had been locked in silence, held prisoner by the self-doubts and fears our father had drilled into him. The spark that started our family drama was Max's stutter. The more our old man tore him down about it, the worse the stutter became. Eventually he stopped talking altogether.

That's when I stepped in. I was only a kid myself, but I took over because someone had to. I cared for Max, defended him, and intervened if our father even thought about going near him. I also took on as many jobs as a high schooler could possibly fit into his life as I worked toward an escape. I wasn't just saving for my own, though—I stayed after graduation, living in the house well past the time when I wanted to leave. I was waiting for Max to graduate. When I finally moved out, I took him with me, and we never looked back.

I'd given my entire soul to caring for my brother. And it was clear to me now that he really didn't need me anymore. He was strong now, and he'd displayed so much courage and bravery and independence as he and Lily found their way to each other. So I guess, in a way, the jealousy that attempted to tunnel out of me earlier also had to do with the fact that he wouldn't be relying on me anymore.

There, I'd admitted it. To myself anyway. I'd gone from being Max's only friend, defender, champion, parent, and entire support system, to simply being his brother. And if I was no longer the rest of those things, *then what was I?*

Just the guy sitting there listening to him. He was the guy who, not all that long ago, wouldn't even *talk* to anyone else. And now he was joking with Claire, a person he was meeting for the first time tonight. *Joking* with her! That joke, when it slid out of Max's mouth and landed with a sly pop in the middle of our group, was the reason I knew I wasn't needed anymore. My focus, the thing that had driven me furiously for years with intensity and zeal as it burned inside of me and guided my every thought and decision, was gone.

Lily had been confessing to Claire that she'd been mugged recently, something she hadn't really told anyone who wasn't my brother. Max had saved her, getting himself slashed with a knife in his successful effort to chase the mugger down and retrieve Lily's purse. Astonished, Claire made a superhero reference, asking if he had a closet filled with caped outfits, each with an "S" on the chest.

"For wh-what? S-stutterman?" Max asked with a wink for Claire. "Is th-that my alter ego?"

"*Superman!*" Lily said, elbowing him as Claire added, "Dude! Come on! Superman would kick Stutterman's butt!"

He told a joke. About his stutter. To a stranger.

That was the moment my brain started melting down, because nothing could have shocked me more. I mean, you know, it wasn't news at all to me that Max was funny—he'd been busting on me for years. He was an artist at it, really. But the fact that he'd joked with a relative stranger was mind blowing. Even his smiles had been treasures so rare that I could probably count them individually. But now? They were becoming his default facial expression.

So…yeah. Max told a self-deprecating joke. And in that joke, I learned everything I needed to know: I'd done my job. We'd reached our goal. My little brother was doing just fine.

And where did that leave me? Tyrone was partying. Max was in love. Mom was floating on a raft in the middle of a pool of denial.

And me? Well, I guess I needed to find some time to mow my parents' yard.

Chapter 3

The Rehearsed Speech

HOSPITALS HAVE the unique ability to overwhelm all of your senses at once. Sounds, smells, sights…I didn't know which to settle my focus on first as the beeps and antiseptic odors battled for my attention as the workers rushed by in their color-coded scrubs. Even as I was standing there in the hallway, a stranger lost in the bustling daily rhythms of the place, I guess my emotions were pulling ahead in the race to overwhelm me, because the dread that had settled heavy and deep in the pit of my stomach was threatening to bring me to my knees. I was standing on the beach, and an emotional tidal wave had just reached the shore.

The gradually increasing numbers on the doors told me I was almost to my destination. I wish I could say that I ignored that emotional tidal wave as I bravely battled the dread, straightened my back, and marched directly toward Room 612. But there wasn't much that felt like bravery floating around inside me that day. Guilt? Yeah, guilt was there. And then remorse and its close buddies, sadness and self-doubt? Yup, they were also present. But bravery? Nope. No way.

I timidly shuffled forward again, afraid of catching the attention of one of the bustling hospital employees. After all, I had no right to make my way over to Room 612. I surely wouldn't be welcomed there. Even the police officer in charge of the case had cautioned me to keep my distance. And the lawyer had all but *forbade* me from going there. Yet there I was, creeping toward that door, terrified but resolute. I didn't know much else when it came to my life, but I knew this: Walking into that room was something I *had* to do.

I hesitated again when I reached the door. Should I knock? Knock and wait? Knock and push my way in, uninvited? Skip knocking altogether? Since the patient in question was in a coma, it's not like he'd be answering the door to greet me, after all. And even if he could, he'd likely slam the door in my face anyway. So, yeah, I wasn't here for a tea party, and etiquette wasn't my biggest concern. Barging in really seemed like the only way forward.

I squeezed my eyes closed, giving the doubts in my head a chance to rail and scream, then I popped them open again, took a deep breath, and knocked.

"Hello?" I said quietly after pushing down on the lever and moving the door forward slightly. When I didn't hear an answer, I jumped into the rudeness of what I was doing fully, pushing the door even further and then slipping inside.

I expected to find the man surrounded by his family members, each one prepared to toss me out of the room again. I also thought I'd encounter hospital staff diligently checking vital signs or adjusting IV fluid levels. What I never dreamed I'd find was exactly what I witnessed as I pushed fully into the room: He was alone. This man, severely injured and broken, just lying there...by himself. Where was his dedicated support system? Where were his courageous defenders?

The shock of finding him alone froze me inside a bubble of indecision. *I should leave. This is crazy. Why did I do this?* Doubts fluttered through my head like confetti as my indecision stretched out, which gave my feeling of dread plenty of time to start frolicking around with its old pal anxiety.

I shouldn't be here. Everyone told me not to come. They were right.

A television turned on in an adjacent room, and the sound was startling enough to snap me out of those spiraling fears. I took a deep breath and tried to reaffirm some pieces of the determination and drive that had propelled me inside his room in the first place. *I've come this far; I may as well see it through.*

I crept toward his bed as the words I planned to say floated out of my mind. I'd been thinking of this moment and practicing a monologue for a while now, one that I'd convinced myself was so meaningful and deep that it could be featured in any of the great classics of literature or stage. But I found, as I finally reached him and looked down into the face of the man who killed my husband, all those words had disappeared. All I had left inside me were wispy emotions, too vague to name or categorize.

As I studied his face, his skin waxy and pale, my thoughts bounced around. I thought about this man's family, and how they must be suffering as his coma was stretching out from days to weeks to months. I thought about my son, Liam, who at seven years old wasn't going to end up remembering much about his father. I thought about myself, widowed by a drunk driver and left alone to raise a young child. And I thought about Dan, the man I'd fallen in love with in high school and married right after graduation. Memories of the time we'd spent together passed through my mind like a slideshow, ending with a vision of his closed coffin at the funeral. His life had been cut so very short by the man I was looking at now, who seemed so vulnerable and small in that bed. It was a jarring mismatch with the powerful impact he'd had on my life.

I held a vision of the husband and father that Dan had been in my head as I leaned forward until my lips were right by the man's ear. My practiced speech was still forgotten, but I knew the heart of what I wanted to say. In the end, I only whispered two short words to him.

"Thank you."

Chapter 4

Unexpected Visitor

"NOW YOU'RE f-finally free."

Max's off-hand comment to me was still echoing through my mind as I drove away from the restaurant, the route to my next destination so familiar that my truck likely could've taken me there on its own. Which was good, considering my mind was still back at the restaurant.

When I hadn't jumped on Max's comment about my freedom with an enthusiastic affirmation or even a joke, I'd apparently set off alarms for him, because I watched as concern wiped all other emotions right off his face. The goofy jokester immediately morphed into my protector—a role-reversal I wasn't so lost in my own worries to notice or appreciate.

"J-Jake? Wh-what is it? What's wrong?"

"Nothing. Everything's great," I said, the lie rolling out with ease. I'd been hiding everything from Max for so long that I no longer had to work at it. "Really."

"I d-don't believe you," he said. "C'mon J-Jake. You've been there for m-me my whole life. L-let me do the same for you. Talk to m-me. Something's on your m-mind."

I was tempted to open up to him, I really was. After all, hadn't I just spent an entire evening thinking about how my brother didn't need my protection anymore? But old habits die hard and all that. Plus, I really wasn't ready to see his newfound happiness melt away so soon after it appeared.

"Maxwell, let this night be about you and your beautiful girl," I said. "Don't worry about me."

"You're f-freaking me out r-right now," he replied immediately. "Are you s-sick? Is it s-something like that?"

"No, man, chill out. I'm healthy as ever." I was rattled by his perception. I mean, *I* wasn't sick, but...I shook off that thought and added, "Really. I've just...okay, yeah, you're right. It's true that I've got a few things on my mind. But that's it."

"Really?"

"Yeah. You know, truthfully, I've been thinking about talking to you and Mitch, but...well...I can't. Not yet."

Mitch was our other brother, and my identical twin. When everything went down with the old man's treatment of Max, Mitch, angrier than ever, moved away to California. Meanwhile I was a one-man juggling act, keeping the spinning plates and rings of fire flying in the air above our dysfunction like a circus acrobat. Mitch, on the other hand, tapped out of the drama. Mom had checked out mentally, too. Max, understandably, hadn't been in any position to help me shoulder any of our family's burdens. So everything fell on me. All of it.

"You'll c-come to me when you're r-ready? Promise?"

"Promise," I assured him—because yeah, eventually I needed to loop my brothers into the nightmare I'd been dealing with for way too long. But not now. Not with his beautiful girl standing there waiting for him and love sparkling in the air like pixie dust.

Someday. But no, that wasn't the day for it.

I parked my truck in the visitors' lot and leaned forward until my head was resting on the steering wheel. My eyes closed, I simply let myself be silent and weary for a long moment.

I'd been shouldering so much that I'd had to develop some coping strategies along the way. What I found is that survival meant I couldn't slow down. I couldn't ever let myself rest or drop my guard. I had to stay ahead of it, or everything was going to catch up, tackle me to the ground, and drag me off to a place where I'd no longer be able to function. I couldn't take my foot off the accelerator, not even for a minute, not if I was going to keep up the pace I'd maintained for so long.

But as I gave myself that tiny treat, that small moment of quiet rest in my truck, I had to wonder if any of that was even true anymore. Yes, I had a lot of responsibilities, but Max had been my main focus during all of it. Nothing else mattered to me as much as he did. But now that he seemed to have made it through the fire and emerged victorious, was it possible that maybe I could slow down a bit? Did I really need to keep running at such a furious pace? Was it even possible?

Maybe….

My mind whirred with possibilities, but doing something as simple as going on a date or even lying on the couch doing nothing seemed equally as preposterous as it seemed enticing. Still, I grabbed a minute more to roll that idea around in my head and examine it from every angle.

Not yet, I finally decided, shutting down my thoughts as quickly as I'd shut down Max's attempts at drawing me out.

I've been struggling alone for a long time. I can make it a bit longer.

With that thought propelling me forward, I climbed out of the truck and trudged into the building, signed my name at the visitors' desk, and made my way through the now-familiar maze of elevators and corridors.

As I finally reached my destination, pushing through the door, I was expecting to find the room quiet and still as usual. But a nurse was there instead, her cheerful words cluing me in that she wasn't the only unexpected person in the room.

"There he is now!" Carmen said. She worked the evening shifts and therefore saw me often. "Hey Jake, your dad's got a visitor."

I waved in silent greeting to her as my eyes drifted across the sheets that covered my father's form. A young woman who'd been sitting at his bedside rose, her worried gaze meeting mine. I couldn't see the color of her eyes, but I *could* see they were deep pools of swirling emotions. I can't explain how any of this is possible, but I easily identified those feelings because it was like looking in an emotional mirror. All the weight of responsibility and weariness I was feeling was right there, heavy and stark on her face. This was a person who knew pain. This was someone with grief and burdens. Somehow, I knew as fully as I knew my own name, standing in front of me was someone who'd understand all I'd been through. It was an odd conclusion to reach based solely on the pain I thought I saw in those eyes. And yet I would've bet all I had at that moment that I was right.

"Hey," I said finally, feeling off-balance and more than a little raw.

"He's the same, sweetie," Carmen said as she finished her tasks and gave me a small, rueful smile. "But you let me know if you've got any questions or if you think he needs something."

"Sure, thanks," I replied with an absentminded wave, my eyes still riveted on the petite brunette, who looked a little like she was about to topple over. I fought back an odd urge to rush across the room and scoop her up in my arms.

"Are you okay?" I asked. "You look a little unsteady."

"I…no, I'm not. Okay, that is," she said, a sharp laugh falling from her mouth even as she reached down to grab her bag from the bedside chair. "But I *really* shouldn't be here."

"Wait…are you…."

I paused then as my brain frantically tried to make sense of her presence in my father's hospital room. As far as I knew, he hadn't had any visitors who weren't me or, occasionally, my mom. My dad hadn't exactly endeared himself to many people in his years on the earth. Suddenly, though, a potential answer popped into my head and out of my mouth before I could even stop or censor it.

"Umm…does my dad have another family or something?"

A wide-eyed look of shock was her only reply.

Chapter 5

A Friend

ANOTHER FAMILY? He'd just asked me…what? If I'd been *dating his dad?* Or, wait…was he asking if I was his dad's secret kid? Is that what he meant?

Why would he ever think that? I wondered as my mouth flopped open from the shock of his bizarre question. I snapped it shut again as I debated how to answer.

"What?!" I finally said, my thoughts no clearer. "I'm not…no. I mean, not that I know of, anyway. Like…as far as I know. You know…that we're not…related?" Burning heat crawled up my cheeks like a spider in a horror movie, and I silently prayed a sinkhole would open up and swallow me.

You know that facepalm emoji, the one that perfectly expresses *Holy crap I'm dorky and awkward* as if that combo were an emotion? That tiny picture floated through my mind as I lingered there allowing random and garbled nonsense to fall out of my mouth. I was being confronted by the son of the man I'd just thanked for killing my husband, and all I could do was babble.

It wasn't bad enough that I knew I'd been caught trespassing or that his question had so surprised me that I didn't know what to make of it. What was truly throwing my brain's ability to form a coherent response into a blender was how astonishingly beautiful the man was. He was all muscles and tattoos and long hair and brown skin. He looked like one of those guys posing bare-chested for a firemen's charity calendar while holding a kitten. He made me want to run into a burning building and wait breathlessly for him to carry me back out.

Hottie McFireman smirked at me, then stuck his hand out.

"Let's try this again," he said. "I'm Jake Cruz, and that's my dad lying there. And you are...?"

He raised his eyebrows expectantly, making him somehow even more attractive than I already thought.

I reached out my hand, then watched as his fingers wrapped around mine, engulfing them in his considerable warmth. *Even his hands are sexy,* I observed silently as I looked up to meet his gaze again.

"Melody," I said, watching him closely now to see if he'd recognize the name. "Melody Harper."

"Melody...Harper...." he repeated slowly, forehead creasing and eyes narrowing. Even though I'd only just met him, I could see that the wheels were spinning wildly in his mind. He'd heard my name before, I was sure of it then. "Harper! Wait, are you *Dan* Harper's...wife? Wait, you are, *aren't* you? You're the widow?"

"You just made me sound like a Batman villain," I said, nerves pulling a dumb joke right out of me like a ticket at a deli counter. "The Joker. The Riddler. The Widow...."

"No, geez, I'm sorry," he replied, embarrassment and confusion lining his handsome features and tingeing each word. "Of course I didn't mean that, and I definitely said it awkwardly. You've got me off-kilter here. But wait, I have to ask—did you come here to pull the plug on him? Yeah, I guess that's a pretty hardcore villain move, right?"

"What?!" I cried, tugging my hand back now. "No, you've got it all wrong! Really, I swear!"

"And I'm supposed to just accept the word of a Batman villain at face value?" he said, his joking words at odds now with his serious tone. "But I don't know why you're joking around with me here. That man right there in that bed is the reason your husband *isn't* here right now, right? You came to tell him off? Serve us with court papers? Something like that?"

I swallowed hard, my emotions twisting my thoughts and trapping them in my throat. To truly explain why I was in that room would mean ripping open the dark box that held my most venomous secrets and shame. Could I do that? *Should* I do that? In a way, I wanted to. In some ways I *needed* to. But I just wasn't sure.

"No, I just...I...um...."

"Listen," he said, finally breaking the silence between us that had descended like a thick fog, "say what you need to say. I can take it. Really. Whatever hate or anger you've got trapped inside you about what he did, let it out. Don't let those sorts of things go unsaid. It's not healthy. And he doesn't deserve your silence anyway."

"You *really* don't understand," I said, shaking my head now. "I swear that's not what this is about. That's not what I need."

"No? Then what *do* you need?" he asked, his voice a husky whisper now.

"Can we go somewhere to talk?" I asked, surprising us both. I hadn't known that I was going to ask him this until the words were already in the air between us. "Honestly, what I need more than anything right now is a friend."

"Funny coincidence," he said, extending his hand to me again, "because I could use one, too."

Chapter 6

The Diner

I FOLLOWED HER car to a nearby diner, my thoughts an anxious, tangled knot. Why would she want to visit my father? If she wasn't there to blast him straight to the inner circles of Hell, then what possible reasons would compel her to sit there alone at his bedside? Her reasons were especially murky since his injuries and sustained coma might forever prevent him from giving her the apologies and explanations she deserved. Wouldn't looking into the face of the monster who ripped your spouse right out of your life be an emotional torture chamber? Why would she have entered it willingly?

There was so much I didn't understand, but there was also so much she didn't know, either. As I flipped on the turn signal and waited for a break in traffic, I wondered if any of that knowledge would ease her burdens. On the other hand, maybe it would do even more damage to her grieving heart. Would it help her to know that my dad was a miserable waste of oxygen long before the night he'd tossed back an ocean of beer and climbed behind the wheel of his car? Her husband was the first person my dad had physically killed—that I knew of, anyway—but he was far from his first *victim*. Would knowing that be a balm on her soul or would it rip wider the wounds that surely hadn't yet even begun to heal?

We slid easily into spots in the diner's half-full

parking lot. I turned the truck off and thought how barely an hour ago I'd sat behind the wheel and tried to grab a moment of rest. I'd actually been stupid enough to wonder if life was easing up on me; I'd even considered slowing my pace a little. The universe's response to that had been swift and brutal, sending me straight into the path of a woman who likely was preparing an ironclad lawsuit that would strip my mother of her house and any funds my parents might have been able to save for retirement. Those problems would then become *my* problems, because that's how things rolled in my family.

So, yeah...I wouldn't be slowing my pace or easing my stress anytime soon. Sure, Max was no longer my main focus or concern. But—*hey, thanks universe!*—now I had this beautiful, fragile-looking woman to worry about. A sharp pain knifed through my stomach at that thought, reminding me that I needed to go see the doctor soon. Just another item on my long list of troubles.

I opened the door of my truck with a long sigh and climbed out, watching as Melody did the same from her own vehicle.

"Hey," I said, locking the truck with the beep of the remote as I joined her. "Ready for that talk?"

"Yeah," she said, her fingers picking at the strap of her purse. "Thank you for this. I...I know it's weird."

"Lots of stuff in my life is weird," I said, trying to loosen her anxious body language with a joke. "Welcome aboard the crazy train."

A quizzical look crossed her face as she studied me a long moment, her hands finally going still from their nervous twisting. I have no idea what answers she found as she looked at me, but I could see the moment she decided to let go of a worry or two and trust that I wasn't the enemy. It occurred to me that this was quite a leap of faith she was taking. After all, what was I to her? The spawn of the evil that destroyed her life? And yet there we were, walking into a late-night diner, a comfortable silence tucking itself around us like a warm blanket.

*   *   *

We placed our orders without either one of us picking up a menu. She got eggs and toast, but since I was currently sitting in my second restaurant of the evening inside of two hours, I only asked for tea.

"I know that my presence in your dad's hospital room makes no sense to you," she said as soon as the waitress walked away. "And…well, I truly appreciate that you're patiently playing along here."

"Playing along with what?" I asked, studying her face more closely now that I could see her in better lighting. She had golden brown hair, hazel eyes, and a small smattering of barely-there freckles on pale, soft-looking skin—skin that I had the sudden and ridiculous urge to reach out and touch. The dark smudges under her eyes told the story of a woman whose burdens were overtaking her ability to sleep, and that only strengthened the magnetic pull that had latched onto me in the hospital. I could sense that we were the same, she and I—in our pain, in our burdens, and in our weariness. We'd still barely spoken, but I felt a certainty about these conclusions so strong that I didn't feel the need to vocalize them. They were there. They existed. They were real.

"Playing along with this," she said, waving her hand between us. "This. Us. Talking. I just don't have…the…."

She trailed off then, as though mere words were inadequate to capture whatever she was feeling and whatever she was trying to tell me.

"Melody, I've got all the time in the world right now," I replied, hoping to find the perfect combination of words to draw her out. "Talk to me. What brought you to the hospital tonight? If you weren't seeking vengeance on my dad, then I honestly can't even guess."

"It wasn't vengeance," she said, shaking her head as she played with the edges of the paper placemat in front of her. "I just needed to see him. To tell him what I had planned out to say."

"Okay...." I nodded and watched her fidget. She had a fussy manicure that didn't seem to match the rest of her look, and this intrigued me. Her clothes were casual, and she wasn't wearing makeup. She seemed like a relaxed, natural beauty, and a woman comfortable in her own skin. But those fake nails with their gleaming red polish seemed a mismatch to the image she was projecting. "And did you? Were you able to get whatever you needed to tell him off your chest?"

"Sort of," she said as she looked into my eyes. "I told him the essence, anyway. Truthfully, all the words I had practiced fell right out of my head as soon as I saw him."

"Okay, so let me guess," I began. Then the waitress came with our drinks. When she left again, I sat back and studied her a moment before continuing. "Let's see, did you say something like, 'Mitchell Cruz, you ruined my life. You getting to lie around in a coma is too easy a fate for you. But hey, I'm a nice person, so I'm glad you didn't die too.' There, how'd I do?"

She shook her head and took a deep breath before

looking me straight in the eye again.

"No, really, you're not hearing me. You've got it all wrong. I *didn't* come to lay blame at your dad's feet for killing my husband."

"You didn't?" I asked somewhat inanely. To be fair, she'd said some version of that before. I guess I just hadn't been paying enough attention. "What *did* you say to him?"

"Thanks," she said simply, sitting back now too and taking her turn at studying me as my mouth fell open.

"That's right," she went on after realizing I was too shocked to respond anytime soon. "I *thanked* him."

Chapter 7

Learning About Liam

"*THANK YOU?!*" I said, the stunned question coming out right as the waitress passed by, the coffee pot in her hand an open refill offer to Melody.

"You're welcome?" the waitress said, a confused smirk on her face now as Melody declined the refill for coffee she hadn't yet touched. "Your eggs will be out soon, honey. Let me know if I can get you folks anything else."

A soft smile had momentarily danced across Melody's face as she watched her go, but it vanished as she turned her attention back to me.

"Yeah," she said, reaching for the little dish of plastic cream containers and turning her attention to the coffee she'd been ignoring. "You heard me right."

"Um, okay...then I guess Dan wasn't a good husband?" I asked as the possible implications of her words spun through my mind like a roulette wheel of misfortune.

"No he wasn't," she replied immediately, her gaze now set on the spoon she was using to stir the coffee. "He hadn't been, not for a long time. The way he treated me was one thing, but...well, I don't know if you know this, but I have a son, Liam."

I waited for several long moments, willing her to continue and yet dreading whatever she was about to say. But when it became clear that she wasn't adding anything to the end of her statement, I decided to break the heavy silence.

"How old is he?"

"Seven," she said, finally looking back up at me. "Old enough to remember, unfortunately."

Old enough to remember.... Just like the way Max remembers every cruel taunt my dad ever uttered. Yeah, I got it.

I blew out a slow exhale, as I tried to find just the right words. Suddenly I was walking a verbal highwire. What she was telling me was heartbreaking, but her matter-of-fact manner was equally disconcerting. She was either an almost unimaginably strong woman, or she was so skilled at burying her emotions that what I was seeing was the beautiful mountain and not the volcano.

"Okay, tell me about Liam," I said finally.

"He's such a great kid," she began, shaking her head as if in disbelief. "Great despite everything he's been through. He's smart, athletic, and funny. And he used to be so outgoing. So friendly. It didn't matter with Liam, and he was kind to everyone. Shy kids. Nerdy kids. Bullies. No one could help it; he was like the mayor of his school. Everyone knew him. Everyone liked him."

"He's not that way anymore, I take it?" I steeled myself against the impact her next words might have on me. "So what happened?"

"Dan happened," she said, pausing as the waitress reappeared to set the eggs and fried potatoes in front of her. Melody continued as soon as she was gone again. "The older Liam got, the more Dan's focus was landing on his son. His impatience and his need to control absolutely everything we did and said. His words and unattainable expectations—all the things he'd been subjecting me to all those years—were starting to shift onto Liam. And the more they did, the jumpier and more fearful Liam became."

I closed my eyes against the torrent of bad memories her words were stirring up. I'd been so right—Melody and I were the same. I knew precisely what she was talking about because I'd gone through it, too. That helpless feeling of watching a grown man target an innocent kid is some of the worst pain imaginable. But I'd only been a kid myself when my dad started his war against Max.

"Verbal abuse?" I dared to ask, afraid of what I was about to hear.

"Not verbal abuse like what you're thinking, maybe. He was strict and demanding. And very jealous. Everything we did, said, wore. *Everything* had to come from him. All ideas had to be his ideas. All decisions were his alone, even down to what we ate. He controlled the money, so he controlled us. I mean…I'm not explaining this well. He wasn't a…monster? I guess. I suppose *I'm* the monster for being so happy to be free, because honestly he didn't get physical with us. At least there's that, I suppose." She shrugged. "But, well, it's true that words can hit as hard as fists."

"Oh, I know," I said. "I know all too well how true that statement is."

"So you have a story of your own," she said, her eyes fixed on me now, a solemn intensity in her gaze.

I took a sip of the tea and used the moment to think about what I was about to say. Was it right to be opening up to this woman? Probably not, especially considering the potential legal actions that were certainly about to splinter their way through our two families. But I looked again at the dark circles on her face and the pain reflected in her eyes. I thought about her son. Then I thought about Max.

I didn't care about the legal ramifications after that. Sure, I'd likely end up caring for both my parents, both physically and financially, for the rest of their lives. But, hey, that was likely happening regardless. She had told me she needed a friend. The truth was that I needed one, too. Desperately.

"If you're a monster, then I guess I'm one, too," I heard myself saying. "You're not the only one who's not especially sad about who that accident affected. My dad's never been in a car accident or taken someone's life before, but your husband wasn't his first victim."

I watched as a sheen of tears pooled in her eyes. She pulled the paper napkin out of her lap and dabbed the corners of her eyes.

"Verbal abuse?" she asked.

"Except one punch aimed at my younger brother one time, yeah," I said. "But I have it on good authority that words can land like punches."

She gave me a rueful half-smile, then settled the napkin back in her lap. She always needed to keep her hands busy, I noticed. Fidgeting and folding and worrying herself into an anxious knot, and I wished I knew her well enough to reach across the table and pull one of those restless hands right into my own.

"How's Liam been since the accident?" I asked.

"I wish I knew."

"He doesn't want to talk about it?"

"No, it's worse than that. And, honestly, it all started some time even before the accident."

"What did?"

"Liam, he…." She paused to take a deep breath

before continuing. "He stopped talking altogether."

The spoon I'd been using to stir my tea dropped out of my hand and clattered noisily to the table.

Chapter 8

Coincidence and Connection

THE UNBRIDLED SHOCK on his face and the pain in his eyes didn't match up with what I'd just told him.

Well...no, that's not completely true. What I said *was* that shocking. And if he'd dropped a thousand spoons, it still wouldn't be proportionate to the suffering that my baby had endured. In telling him that Liam had gone silent, I'd summarized all the evidence in the case I'd been mentally building against myself. I was a bad mom. I didn't protect him. I didn't leave. I'd *failed*.

But this man didn't know any of that. He barely knew me at all, and he certainly didn't know Liam. Also, he'd never been unlucky enough to cross paths with Dan or feel the sting of his relentless criticism and bullying. So I couldn't quite make sense of his over-the-top reaction as I watched him slowly close his mouth and reach for the spoon he'd dropped.

"Good thing it wasn't the hot tea you were holding," I said.

"Yeah, sorry. You shocked me with that, obviously. You couldn't have surprised me more if you'd told me you were a vampire or Liam could fly."

"Why though? That doesn't make any sense."

"Well...I guess you'd have to know where I was today before I made my stop at the hospital to truly understand."

"Okay, I'll bite. Where were you today?"

"At a family dinner," he said. "I officially met my brother Max's new girlfriend Lily."

I waited for more of an explanation, but Jake was sloshing the tea around in his cup, either transfixed by the swirling motion or lost in thought. I felt frustration's grip on me.

"If you think that statement cleared up my confusion, you're wrong," I said finally, working to battle back the snippy tone those words could have held.

"I'm sorry." He raised his gaze back to meet mine and leaned back in the booth again. "I know I'm not being clear here, but you kind of just blew me away, so now I'm trying to get my equilibrium back. And, honestly, I'm trying to figure out how much I should tell you. You're in the position to sue the retirement right out of my mother, after all. And I guess the recovery right out of my dad. Plus, honestly, you and I aren't much more than strangers."

"All that's true, I guess," I said, the eggs I'd managed to choke down so far sitting heavy in my stomach now. "I don't know what's going to happen with the police investigation and the insurance claims and whatever other fallout is currently unfolding. But I'm not actively looking for a cash grab here."

"And I'm not actively looking to talk you out of anything. Do what you need to do to take care of yourself and your boy. But I suppose I shouldn't willingly help you build your case."

"Like I said, I'm not trying to *build* a case." I hoped the truth of my statement rang clear in each word. "I wasn't lying when I said all I really, *really* need is a friend. I don't know why, exactly, but when I was speaking with you earlier, it felt like I'd finally found one."

"I felt that, too," he said. "You know, ever since I first caught sight of you, I've had this sensation that you and I are the same."

"The same?" I asked. "You and *me?* You're not doing a very good job of clearing things up. In fact, you're managing to confuse me more with every word that comes out of your mouth. It's both annoying and impressive."

He chuckled then, the crooked smile on his face one of the most breathtaking sights I'd ever witnessed. Jake Cruz might have the irritating ability to talk like a fortune cookie and wrap me up in riddles and confusion, but there was no denying how beautiful he was. I, on the other hand, am just sort of pale, nondescript, short, and cursed with freckles that make me feel like a child. Me? The same as that gorgeous man? Nothing could be further from the truth.

"I'm sorry," he said, that disarming smile wiped away now. "You've been through a lot, and all I'm saying is that some of it is stuff I'm familiar with. My dad used to berate and ridicule Max about his stutter, until one day Max stopped talking altogether. When you said something similar…well, yeah, that shocked me."

"Oh," I said, my voice a whisper as understanding started to flow through me. "But Max has since started talking again?"

"Yes," Jake said, nodding his head. "He only spoke to *me* for years, and he developed crippling social anxieties that kept him locked inside himself."

"But you said he has a girlfriend," I said, pain streaking through me at his words, which had painted a lonely future I desperately did not want for Liam. "You said you went to dinner with them."

"I did," Jake replied, a shadow of that smile dawning on his face again. "Max, he's in a good place now. The happiest I've ever seen him. He's in love with a great woman, he's working on his anxieties, and he's seeing a speech therapist for the first time since he was a kid."

"That's wonderful!" I dabbed away some tears I didn't realize were brimming until they started to slide down my cheek.

"No tears needed," Jake said, lifting his hand as though he were going to reach across the table and wipe them away himself. I watched, willing him to do exactly that. It had been a very, very long time since anyone other than Liam had touched me in kindness. But in the end, he pulled his hand back down, and that chance to connect fluttered away.

"Liam *will* talk again," he told me in a tone of complete conviction. "And it won't take years, either. I promise you that."

I looked into his eyes, unreasonably comforted by a promise that—let's face it—he was in absolutely no position to give. I don't know why I was grabbing hold of the promises of this virtual stranger, but I found myself doing just that.

In fact, I could feel my heart already clinging to his words like a lifeline.

Chapter 9

Roadblocks

"I WANT TO MEET Max," she said, reaching for her coffee. Then she paused, the cup suspended midair, before adding, "Well, no, I take that back. I mean, yes, I want to meet Max. But more than that, I want *Liam* to meet Max."

"I agree that would probably be great for both of them," I said, nodding slowly as regrets filled me for all kinds of reasons. Some I could identify, whereas others seemed to be buzzing around my brain but were beyond my ability to grasp or put into words just yet. I certainly wanted to do almost anything to make this woman happy. But bringing Max and Liam together? That was one thing I couldn't give her. "But I'm sorry, we can't do that."

"What?" she said, setting the cup down now, those red nails stark against the cup's white porcelain. "Why not? You think it would set Max back in some way?"

"No," I said with a short laugh. "He's so in love with Lily that I don't think anything could pull him out of those clouds. He's like a completely different person these days. I'm telling you, it's beautiful to witness."

"Then why can't some of that happiness shine on my son?" she asked, hurt echoing in her words. "I can't even guess what the problem is."

"It's a little complicated," I replied. I watched as irritation joined the hurt on her face, which caused another spike of pain to stab through my stomach. I took a deep breath and blew it out as I rolled my head to loosen some of the kinked tension that had taken up residence in my neck. For someone who tried to live a healthy lifestyle, I was a mess.

"Could you please uncomplicate it enough to help me understand?" she asked.

"Here's the thing: I don't know how I'd explain to him who you and Liam are," I said. I was suddenly feeling the full weight of my past decisions and current regrets pressing down on me heavily.

"I know the subject of his dad must be a tough thing for Max to deal with," she went on, "so I get where you're coming from, I guess. But maybe offering him this opportunity to use his bad experiences to help out someone else will be healing for him."

"Yes, I think you're right about that," I said. "It would do a ton of good for Max as well as Liam."

"Okay, so why does it still sound like you're putting up roadblocks?"

"Because I am," I told her, then winced at the look on her face. "And because there's something I haven't told you. There's something you don't know."

"And what's that?"

"I've been going through this latest situation alone. I never told Max about the accident. Actually, I never told anyone. He doesn't know our dad's in a coma, and he doesn't know about your husband."

"*What?!*"

"Yeah."

"Jake, why in the world would you want to deal with this mess alone? I *have* to deal with it alone, but you have a choice!"

"I know, I know. It's definitely not the best situation. But, well, with Max, I just didn't want to set him back or change his course. Once Lily entered his life, he started growing and trying and *living*. For the first time since he was a kid, I had my little brother back, you know?"

"Well…I guess I understand why you wouldn't have told him before, when he was first getting to know her. But it seems like the time is right to tell him *now*. I mean you did say they're in love, right? And wait, does this mean you didn't tell any of your other family members, either?"

"No. Well, my mom knows. But she's been locked in denial about everything for so long that she's a master at it. She's still just fluttering around the house pretending we're all about to walk in the door any second and be a big happy family. As if that reality hadn't been torched in a dumpster fire years ago. She rarely comes to the hospital, I guess because it's too much reality for her."

"That's sad," Melody said. "I'm sorry Jake. And there's no one else?"

"No, we've got another brother, Mitch. He's my identical twin, actually."

"Wow, okay. Your info bombs just keep falling. So where's he? Why isn't he here helping you shoulder these burdens?"

"He took off to California a long time ago. I know he needed to get away for his own well-being. I got it back then, and I even encouraged him to go, you know? He was so angry, and he wasn't heading toward anything good. But I never dreamed he wouldn't come back. It's…I don't know. Honestly, I try not to think about it too much. I don't want to be mad at him. I don't want to resent him. I don't want to feel like the person who should know me best in this world actually doesn't. And I don't want to really dwell on the fact that he seems to be okay with that."

"So that's why you haven't told him about your dad's accident? You don't think he'd come back to help?"

"I guess I just didn't want to give him the opportunity to let me down," I admitted, feeling a little embarrassed at finally saying those words out loud. "If he doesn't know, then I guess I don't have to find out *what* he'd do. Or not do."

Melody didn't say anything to that. She simply slid our dishes and drinks to the side and laid her hands on the table, palms up. I reached over and wrapped them in my own, her pale skin a bright contrast against my darker tones.

Nothing had changed. None of our problems were solved, and our issues weren't settled. But as we sat there together in that booth, her hands tucked in mine, a small feeling of peace flickered inside me.

Chapter 10

Aches and Anticipation

I COULDN'T STOP thinking about the things she'd said. Yes, I mean partly about the points she'd made in favor of introducing Liam and Max. And partly about how I should really tell Max and Mitch about dad.

But mostly I couldn't stop thinking about *her*. Her strength in the wake of almost unimaginable heartache. Her ability to reach out to me in friendship even while standing in the still-glowing ashes of the events that had leveled the life she'd known. Events my own father put into motion.

We exchanged numbers that night, then I returned to the mundane cycle of repetitive steps that constitute the minutes, hours, and days of my life. *Wake up. Make a protein shake. Go to the gym. Work out. Check on Max. Attend to my clients in my role as their personal trainer. Check on my mom. Check on my dad. Go home. Sleep. Repeat....*

But her words kept echoing in my head. Her fingers still felt warm in my hands. She'd touched me that day, yes physically as we sat in the booth and held hands. But it was the way she touched me *emotionally* that lingered in my mind. She'd said she needed a friend, and I confessed that I could use one, too. But I guess I hadn't realized how true that statement was until her presence dragged it into the light and forced me to examine it.

I was around people all day, every day, and yet

somehow always alone. Part of the issue was that I'd been doggedly focused on Max and his well-being for my entire adult life. Not once had I switched that focus onto myself. Yeah, I'd dated here and there, but I'd never come close to connecting with anyone. Certainly not the way I watched Lily and Max connect, like two halves of a heart fitting together and now beating as one.

The other issue is kind of embarrassing to admit, because I know it'll make me sound like a conceited manbaby. But, well…okay, here it is: Once I grew my hair long and got my tattoos and gym muscles, women started treating me differently. They fawned. They made jokes. They made excuses to touch my chest and arms. They snapped pictures when they thought I wasn't looking. Basically, I think the women I meet and interact with now assume I only want to date models, so they either treat me like a human photo op or a conquest, but never like an actual human being with feelings, thoughts, or goals.

Like I said, I know that makes me sound like I spend my free time gazing in the mirror and falling more and more in love with myself. Or maybe like a whiny toddler who needs to find his pacifier. But being physically attractive, for me anyway, has become a barrier. It's a force field that keeps out real human connection, and that's just the honest truth of it.

And, okay, I guess that's another reason I couldn't get Melody out of my head: She didn't treat me that way. She was real with me. She was honest. And when she held her hands out to me? She wasn't seeing the sixpack or my body art. She was offering her comfort to *me*. To Jake. Not the model with the manbun or the personal trainer. I liked that we connected that way.

And I liked that she saw me. I liked it a lot. I desperately wanted to pursue this friendship with her—and I desperately *needed* to.

With that thought bouncing around my head, I pulled out my phone and stared at the contact information I'd saved for her. A couple days had passed, and I was itching to see her again. But at that point I'd settle for simply hearing from her.

Me: Hey, how are you and Liam doing?

When she didn't respond right away, disappointment hit me harder than it really should have, considering the circumstances. I checked my phone every couple seconds for a while, but eventually I had to push her out of my mind so I could get through my afternoon appointments. I take my job seriously, which means trying to avoid distractions as much as possible is important. My clients need me to focus on them completely. I have to remember their physical limitations as well as their goals. I never want to be the reason someone gets injured or discouraged because I pushed them too far and too fast.

So it was a happy surprise later when her reply arrived that evening as I was assembling a haphazard salad out of the random contents of my refrigerator.

Melody: Hey back! Yeah, we're okay. One of us is worried and one of us is silent. So...the same.

Me: You two have been on my mind a lot. I know you want Liam to meet Max. But can I meet Liam first?

Melody: Sure. Of course.

Me: I'm still thinking about when and how to tell Max about dad. I don't want to burst his happiness bubble, you know?

Melody: Yeah, I get it. But I'd like to meet Max, too. I want to see what a happy outcome looks like.

Me: You're going to see your own happiness, too, you know. Don't forget about that. But yeah, Max's is something special.

Melody: Want to come over now? Are you busy? We finished dinner. He did his homework. We're just hanging out.

Me: I'd love to, sure.

She sent me her address, and I looked it up on my maps app while I tried to finish my uninspiring salad. It was dry except for the lemon juice I squirted onto it. Dressings all seemed to upset my stomach these days. Then again, it didn't take much to ignite the burning sensations lately. Sometimes they seemed tied to food, and other times stress seemed to light the fires. Sometimes it was my stomach messing with me, but occasionally it felt more like soreness in my back. Sometimes it was after a meal, and then there were nights when I couldn't find a way to get comfortable or avoid the pain as the sleepless hours ticked by.

I was in my late twenties and in peak physical condition, so none of it made sense to me. I shouldn't be dealing with stomach aches and back pains like some world-weary retiree. Yet there I sat with my bowl of dry lettuce.

I'd been chalking it all up to stress, and I still was convinced I was right. But better safe than sorry and all that, so I'd put "make a doctor's appointment" on my mental checklist for months now, then I kept forgetting. Well, and not caring enough to *not* forget, if that makes sense. I had Max to think about and prioritize. And my job. And this nightmare with dad. And mom's persistent rebuffing of reality. Now Melody and Liam were on my mind, too. My aches and pains just didn't measure up to the rest of that. There wasn't room. And there wasn't time.

I eyed the bowl, still half-full, and thought about Melody again. The thought of seeing her filled me with a fizzy sparkle of anticipation, like the sound a bottle of soda makes when you first crack it open.

I stood up, dumped the salad in the trash, and grabbed my phone again.

Me: I'm on my way.

Chapter 11

Welcoming a Stranger

DAN NEVER would have let me go to a therapist. If I had, then I would have been talking to someone who might encourage me to leave him. Furthermore, there would then be someone out there with personal information about me—and all within a setting he couldn't control. For all those reasons, he *never* would have allowed it. That's how his mind worked. Control and paranoia ruled his every thought, so they ruled mine, too. I couldn't make decisions on my own, go anywhere spontaneously, and talk to other people. And God forbid another man should talk to me. Or look in my direction.

He used to accompany me to every doctor's appointment. When a gynecologist banned him from the room once, he stopped taking me there. I was his property, to control, to clothe, to feed. *His.*

Almost immediately after Dan's funeral, I set up appointments with therapists for both Liam and myself. I went from absolutely no freedoms to all I could imagine in the blink of an eye, but I didn't run out and go on a fabulous trip or treat myself to any luxuries. All I could think about was getting help for me and my boy. Liam and I endured a lot of trauma for years. So it's going to take a lot of time and work to get us back to where we should be, and *who* we should be.

As I sat next to Liam and waited for Jake to arrive, I wondered if I should have consulted the therapist about this meeting. Was I totally messing up here? And was I, the minute I was offered my first taste of true freedom as an adult, already making mistakes? Was I walking away from dependence on one man straight into leaning on another one? What did I really know about Jake? Only what he'd told me. I hadn't done any sort of background check on him. If the nurse hadn't recognized him at the hospital, I wouldn't even have proof of his identity. I thought I knew Dan, though, and look where that got me.

So, was I being gullible again? Was I falling for a bunch of lies? I trusted Jake almost immediately. And why? Because he was gorgeous? Because I was attracted to him? Maybe. Or maybe because I still believed I was incapable of standing on my own.

I closed my eyes for a moment, actively working to swat away the spears of self-doubt that I was flinging at myself. Learning to trust my instincts, according to the therapist, was a huge goal for me. Maybe I needed to start practicing now. Jake had calmed me, and I felt like he understood me. But I still shouldn't completely let down my guard with him. And I certainly shouldn't start *relying* on him. Regardless, I had to admit I desperately wanted to see him again. And I wanted to trust myself enough to allow that to happen.

"Liam," I said, trying to drag his attention off the game he was playing. He ignored me at first, then glanced over when I didn't complete my sentence. "I met a new friend named Jake. He's really nice, so I invited him over here to meet you too, okay?"

A flicker of shock raced across his face. Dan never would have allowed anyone over, so my announcing that a stranger was on his way certainly must have seemed unusual, maybe even alarming. I mentally chastised myself again for not running this past Liam's therapist first. What if my instincts were wrong? What if meeting Jake sent Liam swirling even further down his emotional drain?

My billowing inner turmoil, which was cranking up to a full-blown panic attack, was interrupted just then with a ring of the doorbell. Liam's eyes grew wider as they anxiously sought mine.

"Yay!" I said, trying to sound chirpy and carefree. "There he is now. Be on your best behavior, kiddo."

I stood up and nervously smoothed invisible wrinkles out of my t-shirt as I walked to the door. I peeked through the peephole and shivered as an icy stab of worry spiked through me, followed close by a leap of excitement. Even viewed from the distortion of a peephole, Jake was every bit as breathtaking as I remembered.

Shoving those thoughts and emotions aside, I flung the door open with more energy than was necessary. I desperately needed to chill out.

"Hey Jake!" I said with probably too much enthusiasm. My nerves had switched my voice to an overly cheerful setting, with the dork levels turned up high. "I was just telling Liam that my new friend was coming to visit, and then *knock knock* there you were!"

"Hey Melody," Jake said with a lazy chuckle that somehow sounded sexy coming from him. "Here I am."

I could feel my heart racing a crazy rhythm in my chest, and I couldn't decide if it was mostly due to being nervous about introducing a quasi-stranger to Liam. Or maybe it was more about the fact that the stranger was utterly breathtaking and—I feel the need to point this out for no particular reason—he was wearing a pair of soft and well-worn jeans that looked as though they'd been molded onto him by the gods. At that thought, the red burn of embarrassment began crawling up my face.

"Uh, can I come in?" he asked after I didn't snap out of my foggy jeans-trance quickly enough to avoid having the moment turn awkward.

"Oh...sure," I said. "Sorry, I'm a little off kilter today. Come on in."

He walked past me, through the entryway and toward the couch where Liam sat frozen in wonderment. As they assessed each other, I quickly took the opportunity to check out the jeans again while closing the door behind us.

"So, who do we have over here?"

"Jake, this is my son Liam," I continued, joining them as my heart thumped its erratic beat. "Liam, honey, this is the nice man I was telling you about. His name is Jake."

Liam, eyes wide, simply stared back. It occurred to me then that Liam likely hadn't seen too many men with tattoos and long hair, and that was probably adding to the astonishment I could read so clearly on his face.

"Hi, Luke!" Jake said, ignoring the chilly reception he was receiving. "What's that you're holding?"

"Oh, uh, it's Liam, not Luke," I said, wondering how in the world he'd gotten his name wrong. I'd literally said it not two or three seconds ago. *Twice!* Liam, for his part, was still staring, transfixed, like he didn't know what to make of any part of what was happening. But there was something else in his eyes, too—like he didn't want to miss a second of this, either.

"Let's see if I can guess what you're holding, Larry," Jake continued, ignoring me when my eyes popped open wide as he got Liam's name wrong a second time. "Is it…an alligator?"

Liam's face wrinkled up in bewilderment, shaking his head. Then he glanced down at the game console, as though he wanted to doublecheck that it hadn't, in fact, turned into an alligator while he wasn't looking.

"No, huh?" Jake continued with an overly dramatic *I'm thinking hard now* look on his face. "Okay, let me try again, Lonnie. Is it a…basketball?"

"Jake?" I interjected, wondering again if I'd made a huge mistake in not finding out more about this man before introducing him to my son. "What are you doing?"

"Guessing what Lyle's holding, obviously!" he said. "Wait, I know, it's a banana!"

Liam shook his head once more, although I noticed the apprehension on his face was slowly morphing into something that looked a lot like amusement.

"Is it a brick? No? Hmm…your science book?" Jake rambled on. "Wait, I know! I've got it this time! It's underwear!"

Again, Liam shook his head. And then he did something that caused my mouth to fall open in shock.

He laughed.

Chapter 12

Mama Bear

"HEY, LIAM, can you go get our guest some water?" I asked, watching as he set the controller down and stood up. Then he hesitated.

"It's okay, I'm not leaving yet, Leonard," Jake said. Then Liam nodded and darted toward the kitchen.

"He laughed!" I whispered, my eyes wide in wonder. "I can't remember the last time I heard that sound! What are you, some kind of miracle worker?"

"I told you, I've been through this before," Jake said with a dismissive shrug. "This is exactly how I wore Max down and got him talking to me. I used to frustrate the heck out of him, constantly pretending I had no idea what he was holding or pointing at or wanting. Eventually—and honestly it didn't take all that long—I think he decided it was easier to talk to me than to put up with my stupidity."

"That's genius," I replied, gratitude and appreciation welling up inside me and pushing out my earlier embarrassment while fangirling over his outer beauty. It occurred to me then that what was inside this man might actually be even more beautiful, and that was saying a lot. "Did a doctor give you that advice?"

He shook his head. "Nah, there were no doctors handing out advice when my family pulled into dysfunction junction. And I was young, too. Barely in high school when Max shut down. So I can't exactly swear it's even a wise approach. This is something a teenager came up with, remember. All I know is that it worked on my brother."

"So, wait, your parents didn't suggest this?" I asked, still too blown away to wrap my mind fully around the brilliance that he was trying to make into something simple. "You did it on your *own?*"

"Yeah, I'm the only one he talked to until pretty recently, actually. But don't be too impressed. I think the roots of the idea were just in simple brother stuff. We lived to torment each other, and don't forget there were *three* of us. I'd already had lots of practice being annoying at that point. This was just an extension of the relationship we already had."

"Well, it seems a whole lot more than a simple brother thing to me. Thank you. Really. If nothing else, you've given me a glimmer of hope tonight."

Jake looked thoughtful for a moment, then said, "Listen, I made you a promise the other night at the diner. I promised that your boy would speak again. I wasn't just blowing sunshine at you. I meant it, and I *still* mean it."

Liam walked in at that moment, so I had to turn away to quickly wipe away the tears that had welled up in my eyes.

"Huh, why'd you bring a balloon?" Jake was asking as Liam handed over the water he'd secured.

Liam shook his head in a furious *no*, a smile of delight on his face. Up until about a minute before, his expression had been sullen and downcast.

"Here, have a seat," I said, hastily pulling a heaped blanket off the recliner. Liam and I plopped down in our usual spots on the couch as Jake sank into the recliner. It looked strange to see him there, since its previous tenant had been about as different from Jake as two men could be.

I realized then that Jake was a study of contradictions. From the outside, he was dark and tan and exuding male strength. His features were sharply defined, as though a master sculptor had etched and carved him out of every woman's fantasies. But it was the kindness radiating off him that made him so fascinating to me. His empathy for this quiet boy—whom he hadn't even met before tonight—seemed to form a warm force field around all of us. I could tell that it was emanating from a sincere place inside him, the same place where the concern for his brother had bubbled and churned out a constant, steady stream of love and acceptance for so many years.

Dan, on the other hand, had been driven by the need to control every aspect of his own life and those around him. He even held a dominating control over every single hair on his body: Blonde and fair, he shaved constantly and got consistently fussy haircuts so that he'd never look less than his conception of perfect. He'd been the kind of person who always dressed just slightly more formally than any situation called for—the guy who arrived in pressed linen to the neighborhood barbecue or wore a suit to an elementary school play. He exuded impatience and harsh judgment at all times. In turn, nothing about him compelled others to want to be around him. He was hard and unforgiving, unnecessarily cruel and harsh. He didn't exude warmth, sincerity, or empathy. In fact, he repelled those things—whereas the man sitting in front of us now appeared to exemplify them.

"What kinds of things do you like to do?" Jake asked Liam, snapping me out of the morose headspace where thoughts of Dan inevitably led me. He let a moment of silence tick by and then another. I watched as they studied each other, Liam's face crinkled in a look of anxiety and puzzlement, Jake's open and curious. "Oh, wait, I get it! You want me to guess!"

"Not this again!" I said with a laugh as I leaned over to ruffle Liam's hair. He looked up at me questioningly, and I said a silent prayer that my answering smile was reassuring to him. "I'll give you a hint, Jake: Liam doesn't collect alligators *or* bananas."

"He doesn't? Well shoot, there go my first two guesses." Jake adopted another exaggerated pondering pose. "You like to…juggle bowling balls?"

Liam's eyebrows wrinkled in a look that somehow conveyed both exasperation and delight as he furiously shook his head no.

"Okay, okay, let me try again," Jake went on, narrowing his eyes as he studied Liam. "Umm…oh, wait, I know. It was so obvious that I can't believe I didn't get it the first time. You bake chocolate cream pies and use them as frisbees? No? *Seriously?* I swear I thought I had it that time."

I felt myself relax a little; I hadn't realized just how stiffly I was sitting. I leaned back and tucked my feet underneath myself as Jake's guesses kept peppering Liam. The goofiness of the moment suddenly felt so big and important to me. I hadn't been able to give Liam a family environment that provided the things that all children desperately need, like security and comfort. But he'd also been deprived of silliness and laughter. Jake could give him those things, clearly.

With the zeal of a thousand mother bears looking out for their cubs, a feeling of fierce protectiveness surged inside me. This friendship with Jake may not have been preapproved by the therapists. It might be frowned upon by the lawyers and insurance companies.

And society in general might be horrified that I introduced my son to a family member of the man who killed his father. Yes, all of that might very well be true…but I knew then, as Liam's giggles rang out for the second time that evening, that I'd fight to protect this friendship Jake and I were developing.

To my last breath, if necessary.

Chapter 13

Shades of Meaning

I'VE NEVER UNDERSTOOD why my father destroyed our family the way he did. Max had a stutter, but so what? What was so unforgivable about developing a speech impediment? It's not like he *wanted* it. Had my father ever chilled out and just let my mom and the speech therapist work with my brother, I'm sure he could have either eradicated it or found strategies to minimize it. But no, the old man couldn't forgive or accept or simply wait it out, or whatever else he needed to do inside himself to let the situation unfold naturally.

It's because he took the wrong fork in the road when presented with that choice—accept Max or destroy him—that concepts like *home* and *family* and *love* have always been tinged with sad and painful associations for me. If I drew a diagram to show what those words meant, I'd have to create a double helix very much like a strand of DNA, with those darker shades twisting right along with the lighter ones. Even now, woven within the love I have for my brothers, are the pain and judgment and fear we found in our childhood home.

That's what I was thinking about as I sat there in Melody's living room, watching her son giggle. Those two had been through so much—more than she would ever be able to express to me even after a million diner discussions, I'm sure—and yet there they sat together, a united front. A duo bound tight by patience and acceptance. Melody was simply waiting for Liam to work his way through the silence that his father's judgments and eventual death had plunged him into. And yet she wasn't getting impatient. She wasn't berating him or yelling at him. She was merely being supportive and loving. She was giving him the priceless gift of time to find his way through. I'm guessing their illustrations of those word definitions I used before would look a whole lot different than mine.

It made me want the same feelings and associations for myself. If I were in a diner, I would've been saying *I'll have what they're having* to the waiter right about then.

"Liam, honey, time to say goodnight to Jake," Melody said. "It's bedtime, sweetheart."

Liam shot her an impatience-infused, furious headshake, and I watched as a smile tugged at the corner of her mouth.

"Don't argue with me," she said. "Just do it. You know the rules."

With a dramatic and forlorn slump of acceptance, he stood up and took a few cautious, shuffling steps toward me before halting. Then he took the opportunity to inspect me further, his eyes curious and trusting as he took me in.

"Goodnight, Logan," I said. "It was great to meet you. Maybe next time I'll bring my brother Max with me, if that's okay with your mom."

Melody's eyes shot over to mine, wide with astonishment.

"Really?" she asked. "You'll bring him?"

"Yeah. Go ahead and put Lester here to bed. I'll wait, and we can talk more about it."

She shuffled him out of the living room then, and I waved as he turned back to inspect me one last time before disappearing down the hallway.

I didn't lie to her—I *did* want to bring Max and Liam together. Max had come a long, long way, but he still had some growing to do. I was convinced that a mentoring bond with Liam would be huge for him, and the perfect step forward on his journey.

But I wasn't equally convinced that learning about our dad's condition right now would be helpful. Actually, I worried about the opposite: that being forced to think about dad and his coma would be downright detrimental to Max. It might stall his progress or even shove it into reverse. Dad looked pretty pathetic and weak these days, and it was tempting to want to overlook a lot of years of suffering that he'd unleashed on us in favor of pity or even sympathy. Max might feel like the villain in the tale if dad's situation didn't actually make him feel those things. He might even be sucked into feeling guilty or sad or…I didn't know, honestly. Who knew what Max thought regarding our dad these days, if he ever even thought about him at all? I didn't want to force his hand and make it impossible to tune the old man out. I'd shoulder all those conflicting feelings alone and do it happily if it meant Max was safe. I wanted *home* and *family* and *love* to mean different things to Max than they meant to me.

By the time Melody reappeared, I had convinced myself that keeping Max in the dark was the only path forward.

"So…." Melody started as she slipped back into her spot on the couch across from me, "Max? You're ready to tell him?"

"Not exactly," I said, shaking my head as my words extinguished the hopeful gleam in her eyes. I hurried to add, "But, no, I wasn't lying about bringing him to meet Liam. I'm just not ready to take any chances where Max's happiness is concerned."

"Okay...so what does that mean, exactly?"

"I'm just going to say you're a friend and that's it. Pick a place where we met organically—y'know, someplace other than my dad's hospital room—and we'll go with that story. We met, we hit it off, you told me about Liam, I told you about Max, and here we are."

"So we're just friends in this scenario?" she asked as a look that I couldn't interpret skittered across her face. "We're not dating?"

"Nah, we don't need to complicate things," I replied, even as a weird sensation that seemed an awful lot like regret did a bellyflop in my stomach. I had no more idea how to interpret that emotion than I knew how to figure out what Melody was thinking and feeling as she nodded slowly.

"Okay, I think that'll work," she decided. "We're friends, we got to chatting at a diner one evening, and that's when we discovered the similarities between Liam and Max. End of story."

"Right. But where did we *first* meet? My gym? Did I tell you that's what I do? That I'm a personal trainer?"

"Oh, no, I don't think you did. Or I forgot already. But I'm not sure anyone with eyes would believe I spend much time in the gym."

"Gyms are for everyone at any stage of their journey," I pointed out. "But I suppose that wouldn't work. Max meets me there every morning, so he'd probably be able to pick my story apart quickly."

"Grocery store?"

"Sure, okay, that works," I said. "We got to talking in a long line, we went to the diner to talk more, and the rest is history."

"It's not that big of a lie though," Melody reminded me, her demeanor suddenly shy. "I *do* want us to be friends. Real friends, though, not fake grocery-store friends."

"I want that too," I said as happiness surged inside of me. Now *that* was a feeling I could easily decipher. "More than almost anything."

Chapter 14

Treadmill Talk

"WH-WHAT ARE YOU th-thinking so h-hard about over there?" Max asked, his voice yanking me back to the gym, where we were running on the treadmills. He was right that my mind had been elsewhere. Actually, I'd been picturing Melody's barely-there freckles and wondering if she'd ever let me kiss each one. That's a thing friends do, right?

"Oh, nothing really," I said as I lowered the speed to a fast walk and tilted the incline a bit more.

"R-really?" Max asked as he mirrored the slower settings on his own machine. "Is that wh-why you had a d-dopey smile on your f-face?"

"Are you setting up a joke about how my face always looks dopey anyway, little brother?"

"Me?" he asked, fake innocence oozing out of his pores right along with the sweat. "I w-would never add h-here that your f-face was merely d-dopier than usual, so I s-spotted the change r-right away. I'm s-smart like that."

"Mm-hmm," I replied, granting him a side-eye but no further reply as we walked together in a comfortable silence that stretched out for several minutes. It wasn't until we were slowing the speeds and cooling down that he tried again.

"S-seriously, Jake, is something on your m-mind? You know you c-can talk to me, r-right?"

"I do know that," I said, stopping the treadmill

fully and reaching for my towel. Rubbing it over my face and neck gave me a chance to think. It seemed like the right time to bring up Melody and Liam, but I wanted to quickly review our story before launching into it. "Actually, I need your help with something."

"You d-do? Really?"

"Yeah, really." I paused to take a long drink of water before continuing. "Here's the thing: I met a woman named Melody, and she's quickly becoming a good friend of mine."

"You *m-met* someone?!" he hooted, a smile breaking across his face that was so wide I could see every one of his teeth. "Th-this is awesome!"

"I didn't finish talking yet, dummy," I scolded. "Slow your roll. She's just a friend, so get whatever you're thinking out of your head right now."

"You n-need me to b-be your Cyrano," Max said, still fully in teasing mode. But he was also astonishing me once again with his newfound ability to poke fun at *himself*. "I d-do the talking and g-get her to f-fall for you? Something l-like that?"

"I'm starting to regret *getting* you talking again, period," I told him, punching him in the arm for good measure. "You never shut up now."

"S-sorry, Jake," he said, attempting to wipe the glee off his face. "I'm done n-now. T-tell me about her and wh-what you n-need help with."

"She has a son," I said, deciding to get straight to the point, "and he's the one who needs your help, actually."

"He s-stutters?"

"No, but you're close. Apparently his dad was a real dirtbag. Very harsh and controlling."

"Was?"

"Yeah," I said, nodding, "he died pretty recently, actually. Car crash. Luckily, Melody and Liam weren't in the car that day. But at some point, long before the accident, Liam shut down."

"Sh-shut down how?"

"He stopped talking," I said as Max's eyes flew open wide. "Yeah, that was pretty much my reaction, too. Hits pretty close to home for both of us."

"You w-want me to t-talk to her about m-my experiences?" Max asked. "Tell her h-how I started t-talking again?"

"Yeah, sort of. But what I really thought might help is maybe if you'd talk to Liam himself."

"She's okay w-with that? A s-stranger t-talking to her son?"

"Well, she and I are becoming friends, like I said before. You're not a stranger to me, obviously. And I told her how you've totally turned your world around. She's so excited to meet you, and she all but begged me to introduce you to Liam."

"J-Jake, I b-barely got through it, and it t-took me years," Max said. "If it w-wasn't for you and L-Lily, I'd s-still be l-locked up tight."

"Maybe one day Liam will say the same thing about you. You've come a long way, Maxwell. Maybe helping Liam will become part of your ongoing journey."

He looked down as though his sneakers held the answers he was searching for, and I leaned against the wall and waited. I didn't want to push him too hard—but at the same time, I *really* wanted to make this meeting happen.

"I'm n-not you, J-Jake," he said. "I d-don't know if I have anything useful to s-say to a kid. You always knew exactly wh-what to say and h-how to help m-me. I was a m-mess for so l-long. S-sometimes I w-worry it was *t-too* long. That I can n-never really be whole again."

"That's not what I see when I look at you," I told him. "I see a man who never gave up. And a man who is putting in the work it takes to reclaim his life and be a worthy partner to Lily. You were even joking about your stutter the other day at that dinner with Claire. Whether you realize it or not, you've reached the other shore. You're there. So it's time to reach out and help someone else get there, too."

His gaze met mine then, a steely resolve on his face that I'd never witnessed there before.

"Okay…I'll d-do it."

Chapter 15

High Hopes

I *KNEW THAT I SHOULD* be thinking rationally and not getting my hopes up, and yet…. Well, I guess knowing that I should throttle the excitement welling up inside of me and actually doing it are two *very* different things.

So many other things were pushing my battered heart toward that feeling of giddy excitement. It was almost impossible to battle against it. I wanted Liam to start talking again so badly that it crowded out most other thoughts, and that had been my truth for months. But now, suddenly, there were all these signs, like the universe was telling me to just hold on a little longer, and then my wish would magically happen.

The evidence was all around me. It was in my memory of those precious giggles that Jake had somehow pulled out of Liam the night before. And it was in the sparkle of excitement that lit up my son's eyes when I mentioned over breakfast that Jake might be coming again tonight and bringing his brother this time. It was in the coincidence of meeting someone who'd been through something similar, and also in my conviction that Max's story could somehow reach Liam in a way no one else could. It was all of those things— mixed together with Jake's solemn promise to me that Liam would be talking again—that had me agitated and fluttery and glancing at the clock every couple of minutes that day.

It didn't help that I had nothing else to do but wait. Liam was at school, and I was where I always was…tied to the blasted house. Dan never wanted me to work—information I didn't find out until a few years after we were already married. When we met in high school, I talked all the time about how I wanted to be a veterinarian. I never hid that information, and he married me knowing I had those dreams. But since we got married pretty much right out of high school, we couldn't afford for both of us to be in college at the same time. So he went first, after tons of promises that I'd get my chance, too. Meanwhile, I worked at a vet's office to help support us. Mostly I did some receptionist tasks and cleaned up, but they promised to train me to take on tech duties, like cleaning ears, trimming nails, and administering shots and other medications. All the duties that I was eager to learn on the road toward my ultimate goal.

But, of course, reality didn't unfold like that. Actually, most things in my life hadn't unfolded the way I thought they would. So that's the true reason why I really shouldn't have felt too hopeful about Liam finding a miraculous cure via a single meeting with Jake's brother: Things don't work in my world like that. I'm not a veterinarian. I'm not even a tech. I never moved much past trimming nails, and I never got my degree. Outside of Liam and Dan's parents, I don't have any family. Life has largely marched right past me like a parade, and I'm barely even a spectator. I guess I don't know *what* I am.

When my thoughts started driving down the highway of regrets like this, I usually got mad at myself for indulging in the pity party. The truth of the matter is that I allowed it all to happen. I let Dan slowly cut me off from my family and friends. One by one, I saw them falling out of my life and still did nothing. Yes, Dan changed over time. When we were kids, he wasn't jealous or paranoid or critical. But a switch flipped inside of him, and I guess I'll never really know why. And I don't know why I didn't push back on all of it, either.

The doorbell shocked me out of my melancholic spiral. I never had visitors, and now the doorbell had rung twice inside of twenty-four hours. I glanced nervously at my phone to make sure I hadn't lost an entire day, and I tried not to analyze why I was hoping and praying that Jake had decided to drop by hours early.

I battled back the disappointment when I saw the face of Dan's mom through the peephole. I closed my eyes and blew out a breath to steady my nerves before opening the door.

"H-hi, Celeste," I said. "Liam's at school still, but you're welcome to come in and wait."

"Hi, honey, how're you doing?" she asked, swooping me into a tight embrace. "I know he's not home yet, but I wanted to check on you."

"You did?" I asked, unable to conceal my surprise as I pulled back from the hug and shut the door behind her. "Thank you. That's…well…just thank you."

"Liam's suffering, Ron and I are suffering, and you're suffering," she said as she pulled a tissue from the enormous purse she always lugged around. "We may as well suffer together."

"Can I get you anything?" I offered lamely, unwilling to discuss just how *little* I was suffering over Dan's death. "Tea maybe?"

"No, no," she said as she gracefully descended

onto our couch. Everything she did was graceful, and she exuded an old-money aura that always made me feel less than put together. "Just come sit with me and tell me how you two are doing, really."

"Umm...we're okay," I started hesitantly as worries swirled through my mind about exactly how much I should reveal to this woman. She'd always been warm and kind to me, but I'd never let her get very close. This was the woman, after all, who'd helped to create the monster that Dan became. How could I really trust her?

"Liam's still not talking?" she asked as I joined her on the couch. Was she truly worried about him? Or just disappointed that he was less than perfect? Even after all the years I'd known her, I couldn't judge it really, and I didn't trust my instincts in reading anyone connected to Dan anyway.

"No, he's not," I said. "But, well, I might have a little bit of hope building up inside me. I think we might be headed for positive change."

"Oh, but that's wonderful!" she said, reaching over to take my hand in hers. "Ron and I are here for you, and we support you. You know that, right? You can tell me what has you so hopeful. We could use a little good news."

I thought about telling her about Jake and Max, I really did. But then I might have to explain *how* I met them. There's no way Dan's mom would want her grandson hanging out with Mitchell Cruz's kids. She'd never understand, and she'd never forgive me. But I didn't want to lie to her, either. Liam was her only grandson after all, and she deserved to be fully in his life for both the good and the bad times.

I squeezed her hand back as I studied her earnest

expression, her eyes still watery in their grief. I wanted to open up to her…but I simply couldn't.

"It's just a feeling I have," I said finally.

Chapter 16

The Balloon

IT HURT TO LOOK at the unbridled hope shining in Melody's face when she opened the door. It was like looking into the sun, and a feeling of unease and self-doubt rattled through me.

What was I doing getting her hopes up so high? I'd felt so confident when I made those promises, but really, who was I to say what Liam would or wouldn't do? I'm a personal trainer, not a child psychologist. I'm not even a parent.

"Hey, come on in," Melody said, cutting through my inner turmoil. "And you must be Max! Liam and I are so excited to meet you!"

"H-hi," Max said with an awkward wave.

I hadn't really been thinking much about how hard this might be for him. Max hadn't been around too many strangers in recent years. Practically none, really. And even though he'd come a long way, this was still a big deal.

I patted him on the shoulder, one side of my mouth tilting up to let him know that I got it. I alone knew just how hard this was for him. I also knew that his love for me was the rocket fuel that had just propelled him through that door. I hoped he knew I loved him back with the same fierceness.

"Hey, Mel. Where's Leonard?" I said, a full smile reaching my face as a giggle from the direction of the living room met our ears. Another wave of hope crested on Melody's face, which only served to further stoke the fires of doubt raging inside me and wilt my smile. It was going to be a long evening.

"*Liam* is over here," Melody said, gesturing for us to join them in the living room.

"Where? I don't see him," I said, continuing my stupid act from the night before as I entered the room. I scanned the area right above Liam's head as he furiously waved his arms and bounced up and down to catch my attention. Eventually I looked right at him. "Huh, still don't see him. Do *you* know where Liam is?"

His eyes popped open wide at my silliness, and he pointed to his own chest.

"Well, hi, whoever you are," I said. "I'm Jake, and this is my brother Max. Max is a super cool dude."

Max looked over at me, a small panic attack twisting lines in his forehead and furrowing his eyebrows. I nodded my head, and Max studied my face for a moment before inhaling deeply, then crossing over to the couch. He stood next to where Liam was perched, frozen in indecision, as Liam craned his head to look up at him. The two just quietly watched each other for a few long seconds. Then Liam shocked me when he scooted over and patted the couch cushion next to him. Melody's eyes were wide as she shot a gleeful look in my direction. I nodded in response. Yeah, maybe my fears weren't warranted. Maybe we really were onto something here.

"Hi L-Liam," Max started, his voice quiet and quivery. "J-Jake told you I'm his b-brother, but d-did he t-tell you I d-didn't talk for a l-long, long time, too?"

Liam's attention was riveted on Max, a look of puzzlement on his face, as if Max and his unusual speaking cadence were mysteries he couldn't solve.

Finally, he shook his head, as though his brain had taken a few extra seconds to register that Max had asked him a question.

"You p-p-probably noticed r-right away that I t-talk funny," Max continued. "Sometimes p-people make f-fun of me because of how I t-talk. Actually, my d-dad used to m-make f-fun of me the w-worst of all."

Liam's eyes widened, confirming he was processing Max's message, and Melody took the opportunity to shoot another one of her hopeful looks at me. Worry twisted inside, and one of my persistent stomach pains knifed its way through me. *An ulcer?* I wondered even as my eyes moved back to the scene playing out on the couch. *Am I actually developing an ulcer?*

"He w-was really m-mean to me about h-how I t-talked," Max said. "And I was s-sad and embarrassed and f-frustrated. So f-finally I just s-stopped t-talking altogether."

Liam swallowed hard, but his eyes never left Max's face.

Max glanced over at me, and I nodded. He was doing great, and clearly Liam was hooked with fascination at everything he had to say.

"B-but J-Jake was s-sad that I didn't t-talk to *him,*" Max continued. "He used to s-say s-silly things to me and p-pretend he didn't know m-me, just like he d-did with you before. F-finally I realized that t-talking to J-Jake was safe. He w-would never make f-fun of me. He l-loves me and t-takes care of me, j-just like your m-mom loves you and t-takes care of you. You c-can t-talk to her. You can t-talk to J-Jake. I p-promise. If I can d-do it, you can too."

The hope emanating from Melody was filling the room like an expanding balloon, and I said a silent prayer that somehow Max's message would get through to Liam—and that nothing would pop that hope-filled balloon of hers in the meantime.

"He's right, honey," Melody said, crossing the room and kneeling in front of her son. "No one in this room would ever be mean to you. Jake and Max are nice guys, and they understand what we're going through. It's time now, okay? It's time to start talking again. If Max can do it, you can do it, too."

Liam had watched his mom solemnly during her heartfelt speech, but he simply crawled off the couch and into her arms in response. Max's eyes met mine over their heads, the look on his face matching the disappointment I could feel on my own. Liam might start talking again, but it didn't seem like it was going to happen just yet.

The only sound in the room was the quiet sniffle of Melody's tears.

Chapter 17

Planting Seeds

I WAS MESSING UP big time. I'd put way too much importance on a single meeting between Max and Liam, but that was stupid, obviously, and it was way too much pressure on everyone involved. Now my tears of disappointment were freaking out all three males in the room. I tried my best to wipe them away subtly and do some damage control. Meanwhile, I pulled back from Liam and gave the best version of a sunny smile that I could summon.

"Sorry, honey," I said. "I just got a little overwhelmed there. I'm just so happy that we have such nice friends." Then I nodded toward Max, who was still next to Liam, his face crumpled in worry. "Thank you, Max, for telling us the story of how you started talking again, and how love and trust are what helped you the most. I guess we're all just going to have to remember your words while we surround this guy with all the love he can handle."

The cautiously hopeful looks that Liam and Max adopted in response to my manufactured cheerfulness told me all I needed to know about my reaction—that now wasn't the time to wallow in disappointment. No, I needed to remember that all we'd done that night was simply take a baby step on the long path to recovery for both Liam and me. But baby steps were still forward movement, right?

"So did anyone ever find Liam, or what?" Jake

asked, his goofiness fully breaking the tension.

"See w-what I m-mean?" Max asked Liam in a conspiratorial tone. "This guy's s-so silly that I c-couldn't let him b-be the only one t-talking."

Merriment danced in Liam's eyes as he looked over to gauge Jake's response.

"What?" he said, throwing up his hands in fake defensiveness. "I'm the least silly person you'll ever meet. Isn't that right, Lewis?"

Liam nodded in solidarity, then some sort of a lightning bolt idea sent him scampering out of the room and down the hall toward his bedroom.

"Sorry for the tears," I said the moment he was out of sight, finally standing up again. "It was silly of me to think a waterfall of words would immediately pour out of his mouth. The therapist warned me that it might take more time than I was hoping, but…well, you know what I thought."

"Hey, we were hopeful, too," Jake said, a rueful look on his face as he watched me settle into the spot Liam had just vacated. "But this isn't over yet, not by a long shot. Max planted some seeds tonight, and we just have to keep watering them."

"You a big gardener?" I asked, giving myself a reason to chuckle as I pictured Jake in overalls.

"If you saw the state of my parents' yard, you wouldn't be asking that," he said with a chuckle of his own, even as Max shot a questioning look at him. *Doesn't Jake tell Max a single thing about his life or the things he does?* I wondered. Their dynamic was so odd. "It's one monkey-on-a-vine short of an actual jungle."

"You m-mow their y-yard?" Max asked, his irritation coming through loud and clear. "D-dad can't do th-that much?"

Even as I was dying to know how Jake would answer that bomb of a question, Liam came running into the room with a stack of his favorite books from the *Captain Underpants* series. He ran right past Max and me and straight to Jake, an expectant look on his face.

"You want me to read these to you, buddy?" Jake asked, tenderness in his voice and in the look he was giving. "Yeah, I think I can manage that. Want me to move over to the couch?"

Liam looked over to me questioningly.

"I can move, and Max would probably be willing to scoot over," I said. But even as I started to rise, Liam shook his head and turned back toward Jake and pointed at him. I plopped back down in shock.

"You…you want to join me up here?" Jake asked, smiling as Liam nodded furiously in agreement. "Okay, sure buddy, climb aboard."

My tears came right back as I watched my son give his trust to Jake and crawl into his lap. But even though they were tears of joy, I still wiped them away. I didn't want to alarm Liam or make him think he was doing anything wrong. Max shot me a rueful smile, and I returned one with an apologetic shrug. I seemed to be crying about everything lately.

"See?" Jake said as Liam got settled and handed Jake one of the books. "We're onto something here. We just gotta keep watering those seeds."

I nodded and settled back into the couch, contentment filling me for the first time in as long as I could remember.

Chapter 18

Max Weighs In

"Y-YOU L-LIKE HER," Max said the minute we shut the doors on my truck.

"Duh," I said as I reached for my seatbelt. "I told you we're quickly becoming good friends. Of course I like her."

"No, it's m-more than that," Max said, clicking his own seatbelt into place before giving me a look that held a triumphant gotcha-gleam in his eye. "You *like her* l-like her."

"What are you, twelve?" I asked as I pulled away from the curb. Because apparently I'm twelve too, I immediately adopted a mimicking singsong to add, "You *like her* like her."

"I m-may be twelve, but I've g-got eyes," Max shot back, digging in for a fight. "I know wh-what I saw. The m-minute she started c-crying, you wanted to f-fly across the r-room and k-kiss it all b-better."

"Well, I mean…." I started, then trailed off as his words danced around my head. His vision of me kissing Melody's hurts away distracted me, I admit. "Yeah, I think she's absolutely gorgeous. I love how natural she is. And I admire how strong she's been in the middle of an extremely miserable situation. I think she's an amazing mother. And I...um...."

"And you…." Max prompted.

I still wasn't sure where I was heading with that thought. *I what?* In that moment, I had to accept a few facts about the situation. For example, I thought about her all the time now. And I wanted to give my dad an award for removing the abuser from her life. Also, I was quickly falling in love with her son. I wanted to take away all his worries—all *their* worries—and make it so neither of them ever had a reason to cry again. But did that all add up to legitimate feelings for her? Or did I just have the world's worst case of Savior Complex? Maybe this was just what I did now, and Melody's situation would merely end up being a satisfying "fix-it" project for me. I just didn't know.

"And you w-what?" Max asked again. "C'mon, t-talk to me."

"Okay. I guess I *do* find myself thinking about her a lot," I told him. "But I don't know if I have *real* feelings for her, or if I just transferred my need to help someone from you to her."

"Ouch," Max said. "So that's how you f-feel about me, too? A burden you f-feel the n-need to fix?"

"Of course not," I replied, my voice sharp. "You're my brother, and I'd burn the whole city down for you. You know that."

"Yeah," he said, "I d-do know that. But it j-just proves you c-can want to h-help her and also h-have feelings for her."

"I know that," I said, giving up trying to argue the point with him. Honestly, I was so all over the map with my own feelings that I definitely couldn't line up a solid argument in defense of them. "But it's more than just that, Max."

"You're talking about Liam, right?"

"Yeah, he's definitely part of it. I mean, obviously he's great, and he's quickly wrapping me right around his little finger. But his dad just died. Her *husband* just died. I'd be a total narcissist to think I could plop myself right into the middle of their trauma like I'm some kind of reward or something."

"I g-get that," he said. "B-but you said the h-husband was a dirtbag, r-right?"

"Yeah," I said. "He's the main source of both their heartaches. And not so much that he died, but how he acted toward them when he was alive."

"So m-maybe she doesn't have m-much to get over as f-far as her f-feelings go," Max suggested. "M-maybe she needs s-someone to love her and p-put her first after a l-lot of loneliness and p-pain. Honestly, it r-reminds me of h-how I felt when I f-found Lily. She's my s-salvation, Jake. Why c-can't you b-be Melody's?"

"I don't know," I said, shaking my head. "All I know is that we need time. Time for her to heal. Time for me to make certain I know what I'm feeling. And then there's literally finding time in my day. I've just got so much going on. Not sure I can work in a relationship anyway."

"Aside f-from your j-job, what d-do you have g-going on?" Max asked. "All the m-mowing that Dad s-somehow conned you into d-doing?"

"Well, more like *not* doing," I said. "I've been really bad about getting over there."

"Need me to p-pitch in?" he asked, startling me with his offer. Max? Go back to our parents' house? *Really?*

"Are you serious?" I asked. "There's no way in the world you want to go back there."

"Of c-course I don't," he said. "B-but I'd b-burn this city down for you, and I'd even m-mow an overgrown y-yard for you."

I shook my head in wonder at what he'd just

offered. Of course I couldn't take him up on it, since he might interact with Mom and learn about our dad's condition, but the fact that he'd even thrown it out there was twisting my insides tighter than they already were.

"Nah," I finally said. "I'll take care of it."

"Only if you're s-sure," he said. "B-but let me know if you ch-change your mind. I was s-serious. I'd do anything for you, including c-continuing to p-point out that you're obviously c-crazy about M-Melody. You need to g-get your h-head straight about her."

I shot a half smile over at him as his words rattled around my brain. *Was* there room in my life—and my heart—for Melody and Liam? Or was I once again trying to save everyone but myself? I just didn't know.

Chapter 19

Only in Dreams

"HE SEEMS HAPPIER in the last few days," Ms. Wright said. "Lighter, too—like some of his burden is lifting."

I beamed at her, as these comments were some of the best news I'd heard in what seemed like forever. As Liam's teacher, she was rapidly becoming the person I spoke with the most, and our face-to-face updates had become a regular event. Ever since Liam stopped talking, Ms. Wright and many others on the school's staff—including the guidance counselor, nurse, and principal—had immediately formed a wall of support around him. They allowed him frequent breaks, never called attention to his issues, seated him near the friendliest and kindest students, and gave him lots of opportunities to visit them for any quiet-time breaks he might need. Their efforts seemed to be working—he might not be talking, but he was still actively engaged in learning.

"That's terrific!" I replied. "But it doesn't really surprise me, I guess. I've seen a bit of a positive change at home, too. Actually, I meant to tell you this anyway, but he even giggled a few times in the last couple days."

"Wow," she said, visibly stunned. "What had him doing that? Maybe it's something we could replicate here?"

Jake's face, which was never far from the center of my thoughts anyway, popped into my mind then. The image of him reading to Liam the night before was so precious to me. He'd patiently read a couple of the silly stories, infusing them with goofy voices and sound effects like he was recording the audiobooks. Jake was absolutely the reason those giggles had emerged, and I was starting to believe that he alone held the key to unlocking Liam's vault.

"Actually, a friend of mine got through to him," I said. "He pretends he doesn't know Liam's name or what Liam's pointing at or indicating with his non-verbal cues. His guesses get so silly that Liam can't help but react."

Ms. Wright nodded as she stared across the room in thoughtful contemplation. "That's wonderful. I'm going to think about how I might be able to use that information here in the classroom. But it sounds like you need to spend as much time as possible with this friend of yours. If he can elicit giggles from Liam, what else might he be able to pull out?"

"That's kind of what I've been thinking too," I said. "And it's no hardship. He's a terrific friend."

*   *   *

Her words stayed with me through the rest of the afternoon, right along with my own response.

Terrific friend....

Yes, it had only been a handful of days since I met him, but Jake was rapidly becoming my *best* friend. Well, I mean, yes, it's not like I had any other applicants. But even if I had enough friends to form a human chain that stretched to the moon, I had a feeling Jake would still be occupying my number-one spot.

I'd never met anyone like him; it wasn't even close. His love for his brother and his all-consuming devotion to him, coupled with the selfless way he had taken on the burdens of his entire family so that he alone suffered, were what elevated him above anyone else I'd ever known. And it didn't hurt that his beautiful and generous soul came wrapped up with a bow inside a perfectly sculpted body. He was everything I'd ever wanted in a guy, mixed in with a generous portion of more than I would ever deserve. He was kind, funny, gorgeous, and caring, all at the same time. Meanwhile, I was a beaten-down shell of the person I'd always dreamed of being. I didn't have a degree or a job, any friends or family, or even any plans for the future. Yeah, I was a great catch.

I soon began wondering why I was having these thoughts in the first place, though. It's not like Jake had ever expressed any interest in me. Why would he? At most I was a fixer-upper charity project, and I think spending time with Liam and me was Jake's way of bartering with karma. Yes, his dad was responsible for Dan's death. But maybe if he could cajole Liam into speaking again, that wrong would somehow be made right. So that was it, I decided—Jake clearly would never have romantic feelings for a messed-up reclamation project like me.

But the question remained: Did *I* have feelings beyond friendship for *him?* I just wasn't sure.

I pictured him sitting across the table from me at the diner the night we met, his hands gently engulfing mine. Then I tried envisioning how that scene would be different if our feelings were something more. How his brown eyes might sparkle with chemistry-laced interest as I got up and slid into the booth next to him. He might wrap his arm around me and pull me close. And I might even raise my face up toward his, openly inviting the man I loved to lean down and kiss me as I ran my fingers over the artwork that wrapped around his powerfully chiseled arms. The desire between us would build and only be restrained by the public setting. But what if we changed that public setting to something more private?

A bloom of heat rose on my face as the vision turned sultry and supercharged. I reveled in that imaginary tryst a few seconds more, then shook my head and tried to will those dreams to scatter like tumbleweeds across the vast wasteland where my desires lay hidden and dormant.

Yeah, okay, I admitted to myself then, *I seem to be developing a full-blown crush on Jake.* If I was really being honest with myself, I might even admit that I *already* had one. I could also easily envision myself quickly and completely falling in love with him.

But no, I wasn't going there. Ever. Those desires needed to stay locked down. My experiences with Dan had taught me many lessons—and, let's face it, most of them were bad. I'd learned early on in my marriage that my instincts were terrible. And I'd learned there are much, *much* worse things than being alone.

It would be one thing to risk another toxic relationship if it was just me. But Liam and I were a package deal now, and I could never fully trust another man with him in the picture. Not after what Dan had done. My intuition said that Jake would never in a million years hurt either one of us. But I also knew there were no guarantees. And since I couldn't be sure, then there was nothing to decide. Could I fall for Jake? Yes, easily. But could I ever take the risk that went along with that?

Absolutely not.

Chapter 20

Mowing and Mulling

I TRIED TO STAY away from Melody, I really did. That was why I was finally mowing my parents' yard the day after we introduced Max and Liam. What I really wanted to do was drive straight back to Melody's house and hang out with those two again. But in the end, I talked myself out of it. Friends don't smother each other or spend their every waking hour together, right? Plus, I didn't know how tight of a bond she really wanted me to create with Liam in the first place. The more time I spent with the little guy, the more I was going to love him. And he'd likely get more attached to me, too. That could get messy one day when she was ready to move on and find someone to love. The new guy might not want to share stepdad duties.

These thoughts did something inside my chest that I'd never felt before, causing me to stop pushing the mower and take a few deep gulps of air. It was like an icy spear of dread had teamed up with some other emotion I wasn't sure how to label. The bizarre tandem was causing an almost physical ache, and I rubbed my hand across my chest in an attempt to soothe it. But what was I really having this quasi-heart attack about, though? The thought of someone else stepping into the role of Liam's father? Really?

Or was it the thought of Melody finding someone else to love?

Was that the emotion I couldn't identify? *Jealousy?*

Had Max been right that I *"like her* like her," as he put it?

Using the bottom of my shirt as a towel, I swiped my sweaty forehead and then started moving forward again as I continued tossing these questions around in my mind. Max had merely heard Lily's laughter through a wall and had instantly started developing a crush on her. But he hadn't been confused by those feelings. He knew right away how much he liked her, and that he'd love a chance to date her. When the opportunity came along to get to know her, he grabbed it and never looked back. Meanwhile, here I was, after meeting a beautiful and courageous woman, completely confused about how I felt or what I wanted. The irony was not lost on me that Max, after years of locking himself away from interactions with the rest of humanity, was *still* more in touch with his emotions than I was.

As I continued trudging back and forth across the yard, I decided to run an experiment. I pictured what Melody and I would look like as a couple. Instead of sitting home alone every night with my bowls of dry salad and an endlessly scrolling to-do list, I'd be pulling more giggles out of Liam as I read to him in the recliner. Or maybe we'd play catch in the backyard. Naturally, I'd become part of the routine each night of settling him down to bed, leaving the rest of the evening free for Melody and me to get to know each other better. Maybe we'd cuddle on that couch of hers and watch cheesy movies. Or maybe we'd sit out back and watch the stars and talk about our plans and dreams. I liked this vision a lot. After all, I didn't know that much about her yet. We could fill a whole lot of evenings with talking and laughter, and then we could cap them off with....

My brain short-circuited then as the idea of us kissing and exploring and loving each other flooded my thoughts. Would her skin be as soft as it looked? Would it…*no, okay I need to stop,* I thought as I pulled to a halt at the edge of the yard. So, yeah—*I've proven to myself that I'm attracted to her,* I thought as I surveyed my work. Of course I was. She was everything I could possibly want in a partner: She was smart, strong, honest, kind, patient, and an amazing mother. As the cherry on top of all those other amazing qualities, she seemed to see past my exterior right into my inner heart and soul. And she seemed to like what she saw.

I emptied the mower bag and then returned it to the shed, my mind still an unsettled whirl of doubts mixed with yearning. My vision of us was so real that it almost felt like Melody was home waiting for me to come make it happen. But that was crazy. For one thing, we barely knew each other. Also, we each had a mountain of family issues weighing us down; they were issues that, unfortunately, intertwined and divided us into opposing sides. My dad *killed* her husband! If ever there was a hurdle too big to get over, it had to be that one, right? Sure, we were friends. But there was a lot of trouble and a whole lot of pain filling up the divide between us. I just didn't see how we could ever build a bridge across it.

I eyed the edger hanging on the inside wall of the shed, debating whether I wanted to neaten up the yard and do a professional-looking job. Or…*I could just go drop by and see how Melody and Liam are doing today.* There may be a valley too wide to cross between us, but that didn't mean I didn't still want to see her. I leaned toward the edger, even as thoughts of Melody again twisted an ache inside my chest.

With a shake of my head, I pulled back and closed the shed doors, set the deadbolt in place, and headed for my truck. I knew if I hurried home to take a quick shower, maybe Liam and I could play that game of catch before the sun went down. And then maybe Melody and I could get to know each other beneath the starry night sky.

Just as friends, of course.

Chapter 21

Surprise Visit

JUST BECAUSE I'D DECIDED we could never be anything more than friends—and it didn't seem like Jake would have any problem with that anyway, despite a few chemistry-laced moments we'd shared—it didn't mean I couldn't spend time with him. At least that's what I was telling myself each evening as we settled into a nightly pattern of sharing his free time together.

Liam still hadn't said a word, but his feelings about Jake weren't something he needed to verbalize anyway. No one could have missed the attachment that was developing between them. Sometimes they played games, like *Uno* or *Connect Four*. Jake also introduced him to the world of *Looney Tunes* cartoons, and Liam reciprocated with his *Wimpy Kid* and *Captain Underpants* books. Sometimes they played catch in the backyard. And sometimes they just sat together in Dan's...no, *Jake's* recliner. It was now his as surely as he now owned Liam's heart. And, face it, *my* heart, too. And yet...we had to just be friends. That wasn't going to change.

My mind, heart, and emotions were forming little heart-shaped bubbles around me as I watched them sit together reading Liam's favorite *Dog Man* book for the hundredth time one evening, when the doorbell rang.

"You expecting someone?" Jake asked, turning his attention off the book and looking up at me with those sleepy, deep-brown eyes of his. Concern and surprise mingled together in the odd look he was giving me. He had a right to be surprised, of course—we'd never been interrupted before.

"Not that I recall," I said, so taken off guard that I didn't pause to look through the peephole to see who it was. Dan's parents were standing there giving me a look of relief that I didn't understand when I swung the door wide.

"H-hi," I said. "What a surprise!"

"Oh Melody, is everything okay?" Celeste started in, grabbing both my arms and assessing me critically while doing the bulk of the talking for the two of them, as usual. "We tried calling just to say hi, but when you didn't answer, we got worried. And then when we got here and saw an unfamiliar truck in your driveway, we started to get positively frantic!"

"One of us did, anyway," Ron said. "You okay, honey?"

"Yeah, of course," I said as alarm started building pressure inside of me. Celeste and Ron? *Meeting Jake?* "I'm sorry, my phone was on the charger, and I guess it's on silent or off or something. Come on in."

As my brain scrambled to come up with how I was going to introduce Jake to them, Celeste finally let go of my arms. Then they both moved past me and straight into the living room, where Jake and Liam were sitting together in a cozy cuddle, in Jake's—*although to them it was still Dan's*—recliner.

They pulled up short, their eyes wide as they took in the scene before them. Jake lamely lifted his hand in a wave as Liam scampered down and wrapped himself around Celeste. He'd always been closer to her than her quieter husband.

Jake stood up and glanced over at me, mute and frozen in the doorway. Finally, he tried to dispel the awkwardness by reaching out his hand. "Hi, I'm Jake. Jake Cruz."

"Celeste and Ron Harper," Celeste said, her voice wooden and her hand firmly at her side. Just as Jake was lowering his own in awkward resignation, Ron reached out and shook it.

"We're Dan's parents," he said. "And Liam's grandparents, of course."

"Nice to meet you," Jake said, shooting another questioning look at me. I was still acting like a statue, but his look succeeded in pulling me out of the paralysis.

"Liam, can you go get Grandma and Grandpa some water to drink?"

I watched as he pulled back from Celeste, then shot a questioning look at Jake.

"Go on, buddy," Jake said. His words seemed to release Liam from his indecision, and he bolted into the kitchen.

"Jake's a friend of mine," I said after Liam disappeared, wiping my sweaty palms on my jeans. "He's been such a rock for me during the last few months."

"I'll bet he has," Celeste said, her face a battleground against the tears that were threatening to pour down her grief-lined face. "Oh Melody, so soon?"

"To make a friend?" I asked. "I'm serious, we're *friends.* Absolutely nothing more. Of course I know it's too soon. I know that wouldn't…look right. Or *be* right, I guess."

"Really? That's what you think? Well, this doesn't look so great, either," Celeste said as she lost the battle against her tears. "You're telling me that a man who looks like *that* is simply a sounding board for a young and grieving widow. And one who's recently come into a considerable insurance payout, I feel the need to add?"

Jake's mouth fell open. He looked like he was about to defend himself, but when I held up my hand and gestured for him to stop, he did. I noticed, however, that his hands were tightening into fists at his side.

"Please don't judge him by his looks," I started. "He's a self-sufficient, tax-paying member of society who doesn't need a single thing from me. He's too busy lovingly caring for every single member of his family. And he's got a brother who once stopped talking, too. His perspective, and his advice, are invaluable to Liam and me. He's a wonderful man who's shown us nothing but patient kindness. So please try to understand."

"I'm sorry, Melody, but *you* can't possibly understand how hard it is to see another man sitting in that chair and spending time with Liam, time that my child will never again get to spend. Those snuggles in that recliner? They should be Dan's."

Part of me wanted to tell her that Dan had *never* snuggled in the chair with Liam or read to him or any of the other things that Jake did. His idea of bonding with Liam was picking through his schoolwork and questioning each mistake. He used to make Liam redo assignments nightly until Liam was in tears. If he had been here, this wasn't the domestic scene they would have walked into. Not by a long shot.

But I was a mother, too, so part of me understood that she'd never be able to see Dan for who he really was. I'd never told them what was happening, and I'd never trusted them enough to ask them for help. As far as they knew, I *was* a grieving widow.

"I'm sorry," I said. "As a mother, my heart breaks for you. But, also as a mother, surely you can understand that I will do anything, literally anything, to get Liam talking again. He enjoys spending time with Jake. And Jake alone can get him giggling, which I think is wonderful progress. Please understand that nothing you say and no number of tears you cry will ever make me push Jake out of our lives."

Ron simply nodded his understanding at me, although he had to be shocked. I'd never spoken to either of them like this in all the years they'd known me. Celeste's quiet, hiccupping breaths were the only sound in the room for several long moments.

"I can't do this," she said finally, rushing past me.

Ron shot me a regretful look, eyed Jake for a couple of long seconds, then nodded his head and turned to follow his wife out the front door.

Chapter 22

Acts of Defiance

THE CLICK OF THE DOOR echoed in the room, and I chanced a glance over at Jake, not sure what emotion I might find on his face. Anger, I was guessing, since it was my fault that he'd been subjected to that ugly display of upper-class disdain. Or maybe impatience, since I'd effectively cut off his attempt to defend himself.

So I was utterly shocked when instead he met my gaze with a look of pure love and desire. I inhaled in shock, then tried to backpedal when Liam reentered the room, looking around for his grandparents with newfound worry in his eyes.

"They had to go, honey," I said. "They told me to tell you goodbye and give you a million squeezes and kisses, okay?"

He nodded, but my words had done nothing to dispel the anxiety on his face.

"Hand those waters to Jake," I said. "I'll bet he's super thirsty after reading *three* whole books tonight, and let's go get you ready for bed."

He didn't put up much of a fight, although it felt like he lingered in his hug with Jake longer than ever before. Maybe he'd heard more of his grandparents' words than I'd hoped.

When I came back into the room, Jake had switched over to the couch, and he patted the cushion next to him.

"C'mere."

I took a deep breath and tried to gauge if that look that I'd identified as love or passion was still evident on his face. I couldn't tell, and my movements were jerky and hesitant as I collapsed next to him.

We sat in silence while I gathered my next thoughts.

"I'm so sorry about that, Jake. They had absolutely no right to judge you or say those things about you."

"I get that a lot," he said, shrugging off my words easily. "Ever since I grew my hair out and started acquiring tattoos. Some people love body art and find it sexy, and some people find it dirty and low-class."

"Why *did* you get them?" I asked, something I'd never before been brave enough to say out loud, despite the ridiculous amount of time I spent thinking about them. I was clearly in the "find it sexy" camp, at least where Jake was concerned.

"It was something the old man hated," he said, mischief creeping out in the tiny smile he showed me. "He used to talk all the time about the long-haired, tattooed 'druggies' he claimed to see every day at the factory where he was working at the time. He must have forbidden us dozens of times to ever 'mark our skin' that way."

"So you did it to defy him?"

"Yup," he said with a lazy chuckle. "The day we turned eighteen, Mitch and I went and got the gaudiest tattoos we could find on our backs, where he'd be sure to see them. Made him furious, but hey, it was done already, and we were legal adults."

"But you have full sleeves on your arms," I pointed out. "It wasn't just a one-time big display of defiance."

"No, we both kind of fell in love with it," he said. "Ask anyone with multiple tattoos: They're addictive. I regretted the big ugly monstrosity on my back though—it was this ridiculous skull and crossbones with fire jutting out of it. So I slowly had it covered up with a bigger, more complete design that reflects more of who I am."

"What is the image now?" I asked, wondering if he could feel how hot it was in the room as I envisioned him whipping off his shirt to show me. "What reflects the real you?"

"It's an M," he said. "For Max. And the flames are wings now. Who I am is wrapped inside of who and what Max was struggling to be."

"Free?"

"Absolutely. I just wanted Max to be *free*. And in *his* freedom, I hope to find my own, you know?"

I nodded, because of course I understood that. He'd turned his entire life over to his brother, after all.

"Can I throw a personal question your way, too?" he asked.

"Of course," I replied, nervous he was going to try to get me to explain my feelings for him. They were entirely too complex to be discussed casually. Or even seriously, for that matter. Not yet.

"Why the red nails?" he asked then, reaching for my hand. His thumb felt rough across my skin as he rubbed my palm gently. "They don't…look like you, I guess. You know, I noticed and wondered about them that first night in the diner."

"You're pretty perceptive," I said, his words throwing another log on the fire of my confusion about my feelings toward him. "But yeah, I freaking *hate* them."

"Wait…what?" he asked, astonishment ringing clear. "I figured you *loved* them for some reason. I thought that maybe it was rooted in the desire to give yourself a well-earned treat?"

"Nah, nothing like that," I told him, looking down now as he gently laced our fingers together. His touch sent bolts of awareness zigzagging through me. "Dan learned from the best when it came to being judgy, as you experienced tonight. But he took those lessons and went way further with them than his parents ever did. He used to insist that I always have a full face of makeup on each day. He said he worked hard, and he deserved to be looking at a beautiful wife."

"You're the most beautiful woman I've ever seen," Jake said then, reaching up with his free hand and touching my nose with his forefinger. "I'd never want you to cover those cute little freckles. I'm kind of obsessed with them."

"He was, too, but his response to them was a little different. I had to cover and conceal any imperfections and blemishes, or I'd never hear the end of it. Even on days when I was sick. Even right after I gave birth to Liam."

That last comment caused his eyes to lock with mine. He looked like he was struggling with how to respond, and I almost wondered if he was about to say something super possessive and alpha about how he'd never do that if I was *his* woman. But in the end, he simply said, "He didn't deserve you, Melody."

"Thanks, I appreciate that. And I meant everything I said tonight about how you're a permanent part of our lives now. I won't let them scare you away."

"We'll get to that in a minute. You talked about the makeup, but what about the long, red nails? Was that something he insisted on? Have you just not gotten around to removing them?"

"Oh no," I said, my eyes back on the sight of his hands caressing mine. "He hated fake nails and any nail polish other than a simple light pink or French tip. He used to talk all the time about how fake women who wear them are, as though he wasn't, out of the other side of his mouth, forcing me to be fake with my looks."

"So this represents an act of defiance?" he asked, then nodded in approval. "I like it."

"It was one of the first things I did in the days following his death," I admitted, something I hadn't told another soul. "I even wore them to his funeral and spent much of that time thinking about how much he'd hate them."

"You're amazing," Jake said then, shaking his head. "And you're stronger than you even realize. When you defended me so fiercely earlier, it made me think that, well, that maybe you feel—or at least one day *could* feel—the same way I do."

"And how is that?" I asked, the words coming out all embarrassingly breathless.

"Like I'm falling in love with you," he replied.

Then he leaned forward and captured my lips in a gentle kiss.

Chapter 23

Heartache

I KNEW I SHOULDN'T be pushing her; I really did. It was all just way too soon, but her defense of me that night, and her insistence to Dan's parents that I was a permanent part of her life, gave me a sense of *rightness* like I've never known before. Like I was exactly where I was supposed to be, and Melody, Liam, and I were a team. A united front. A *family*.

And yeah, I'll admit that hearing more details about Dan's abuse of her made me furious. It wasn't right that his were the last lips she'd kissed. He didn't deserve that honor.

But more than anything, after weeks of spending time together, I was dying to touch her like that. Every cell in my body was tuned to the desire to connect with her physically as well as emotionally. So yeah, I leaned over and kissed her.

I'm not a caveman, though. I kept the kiss light. And when she returned a few exploratory kisses of her own, it seemed like maybe we were on the same page and ready to move toward being an actual couple. Happiness like I'd never known blossomed inside me. I was finally experiencing my own version of what Max and Lily's love looked like, and I've got to say, the feeling was more precious than I could ever have guessed. This was it—I'd found her. She was the other half of my soul.

So my fall back into reality was a long, bumpy drop

followed by a nasty shock when she pulled away with alarm and misery flashing brightly on her face like a traffic signal gone haywire.

"No!" she cried, yanking her hand from mine as she scrambled to the other end of the couch. "We can't do this, Jake."

"*Yet,* you mean?" I asked, still stunned. "We can't do this *yet?* Hey, I get it. It looks bad for you to move on too quickly. But I would never push you, Mel. We can slow things down until you think enough time has gone by. I'll wait forever for you."

She tore her eyes from mine, her head shaking *no no no* as she stared furiously at those red nails of hers. The silence stretched out until seconds became minutes, but I knew not to push her any further. This had to be her decision and on her terms; I'd be a fool not to get that. So I simply sat there, mute and frozen, as the pain in my chest grew. It wasn't some metaphorical, lovesick chest pain either; I was kind of wondering if I was having a literal heart attack as I continued to watch her struggle with what to say. The more it looked like she was trying to find a way to let me down easy, the more intense the pain got.

"No, I didn't mean not *yet,*" she said finally, looking back up with tears on her precious face. "I meant not *ever.* We're friends, and I don't want anything to mess that up. I can't lose you in my life, but I only want you in it as a friend, okay?"

"Wow, I'm so sorry—did I totally misread your feelings?" I was embarrassed and, frankly, amazed that I could talk after being sliced apart by her words. "You're not attracted to me?"

"Get out of here," she said, a choked laugh escaping her throat as she gestured in my direction. "I mean look at you. No one, male or female, *wouldn't* be attracted to you. That's part of the problem, actually. I don't believe that you would possibly see anything in me. We're not on the same level; we're barely the same species."

"No, Mel, c'mon, not you, too," I said, the pain all but crushing my chest now. "I never connected with anyone before, partly because everyone judges me by the outside. Everyone, that is, until I met you. From that first night in the diner, you always seemed to see past all of that. You've always seen inside and seemed to care about the *real* me. Please don't change that now."

"No, I *do* see what an amazing man you are," she replied immediately. "You're right; I have from the minute I met you. There you were, checking on a father who doesn't even deserve your allegiance. You're special, Jake. One of a kind. You're selfless and loving, and I could never repay you for the time you've already spent with Liam or the progress he's made with you. Not if I had a billion dollars. I treasure you, and I meant what I told Celeste and Ron earlier. I'd fight a tiger to keep you in my life."

"You could stab it with those nails of yours," I said, chuckling in spite of myself.

"Don't think I wouldn't," she shot back, the smallest upturn of her mouth the only visible sign that the tension between us had dissolved a bit.

"Okay," I went on, "so, you *are* attracted to me, and you do value me as a person and a friend...." I was still trying to understand what she was saying, and why she was so insistent that we could never be an *us*.

"You're my *best* friend, Jake."

"You're mine, too, Mel. And I have romantic

feelings for you, but I guess you're saying that you don't have them for me? Is it a 'the heart wants what it wants' thing?"

"Honestly, I don't know," she replied, although the look in her eyes was a mismatch with what she was telling me. Yearning is what I saw there, and deeply passionate longing, which meant she was being forced to deny her true feelings for me. I clung to that look. "All I know is that we can never be more than friends," she continued, "and I'm asking you to be okay with that."

"Well...." I started, then trailed off lamely. *Okay* with it? I'd never be okay with it. But I also wasn't Dan, and I'd never force her to do anything she didn't want to do, even if that meant shoving my feelings down and locking them away forever. "All right, I'll try."

Her face shone with appreciation then, and the look of stressed-out misery seemed to lift, dispelling a bit of the pressure—pressure that I already regretted applying. But, honestly, it seemed to me like the look of intense longing was still there in her eyes, too. Then again, I was so confused about what she was telling me that I was probably way off-base in thinking that. I clearly couldn't read this woman's emotions at all.

In the end, I decided that the yearning I thought I saw shining in her eyes was simply a reflection of my own.

Chapter 24

Tears and Regrets

I DID THE RIGHT THING. I'm a mom, and that has to be my focus. Liam's my only priority. So, yes—I did the right thing. I did....

These thoughts were circling in my brain on an endless loop during the entire painful conversation with Jake. And after he lit every nerve-ending in my body on fire with his tender and loving kiss. Those words kept right on circling in my brain after he left, too, as I sat alone on the couch with only those looping thoughts for company.

With every single fiber of my being, I was absolutely dying to confess to him that yes, of course I was well on my way to falling in love with him. Well, that is if I hadn't already fallen, landed, and gotten the breath knocked out of me by such an amazing man. If it wasn't for how little I trusted my instincts and how fiercely I wanted to protect my son, I would have wrapped myself around Jake like a howler monkey the moment his lips touched mine. I wouldn't have ever let go, either. I hadn't lied to him when I said he was my best friend. But somewhere along the way, he became part of my heart and soul, too.

I think he must have known that's what I actually wanted and what I was secretly yearning for, because although my words were pretty harsh and clear, he looked utterly confused by them. Confused and in so much pain. And that, in turn, was causing me pain. The last thing in the world I would ever want to do was to hurt him, especially after meeting Max and then learning about the miracles Jake had helped bring about in his brother's life. Anyone who'd dedicated himself so fully to the well-being of his brother—down to inking that dedication permanently on his back!—was someone with a heart of gold. And I was taking that heart of gold and melting it down.

Part of me was convinced that Max was my proof that Jake would never, ever hurt Liam or me. That, despite my extreme miscalculations in reading Dan's character, I'd accidentally stumbled across the best man I could ever possibly hope to meet. That part of me was the howler monkey side, desperately longing to latch onto him and never let go.

But I also firmly believed I couldn't be sure. I mean, how could I take such a chance when Liam was still locked up tight in his silence and his trauma? He deserved a mother who was focused solely on him, not on launching her dating life as a new widow. I needed to worry about making sure he had all the stability and love he needed. I'd keep taking him to therapy while hoping Jake could cajole a few more giggles out of him, and then praying for a major breakthrough.

I'd also been toying with the idea of looking for a job. Dan had forced me to quit the vet clinic where I'd worked years ago, so I didn't exactly have a long list of glowing references. But hey, if sixteen-year-olds with no work or life experience can manage to find part-time jobs, so could I. Of course, I could look for fast-food jobs or convenience-store openings or similar places with no degree or experience requirements. But I was tempted to go back to the clinic and see if there were any familiar faces left. If I was really feeling brave, I might even open up and explain what had happened.

I'd have to admit that I'd been in an abusive relationship. I was ashamed of it, but it was the truth nevertheless. The therapist said part of my healing would lie in facing that truth and deciding what I wanted to do about it. Keep hiding in the house? Keep being ashamed? Remain detached from the rest of the world? Or would I start owning my mistakes? Would I choose to begin building connections with the rest of the world rather than remain isolated? So yes, maybe I could get a job. Make some new friends. And have a life again.

I not only wanted those things, I desperately needed the change. I didn't want to stay hidden away forever. Despite forcing myself to detonate any chance of finding love with Jake, I really did want a brighter future above all else.

My mom's face flickered into my mind then, and the automatic tears that came along with any thoughts of her sprang to my eyes. Since I was crying already anyway, I gave myself the rare luxury of letting myself think about her. She had been a single mother just like me. I'd never known my dad—he skipped town the minute the pink line showed up on her pregnancy test. She'd worked hard the rest of her life in multiple jobs to keep me fed and clothed. We never had much, but I knew she loved me and would do anything for me, and that was enough.

She alone had encouraged my love of animals, too. We'd been much too poor to afford pets, but she'd allowed me to worry and fuss over stray cats, the occasional opossum, and even a few raccoons. She brought home Styrofoam containers from work and allowed me to build winter homes in the backyard for them. She didn't even get mad when it turned out that one of my tenants was a skunk.

Even as the memory of that skunk tried to bring a smile to my face, agony sliced through me again, practically doubling me over with its intensity. That's why I generally avoided thinking about my mom these days. I had known how much she loved me and how much she'd sacrificed for me, and still I'd betrayed her. I'd broken her heart with a devastation of such magnitude that it would be a joke to try to compare it to the heartache I might have caused Jake earlier that evening. After all, I was the reason my mom had died of a broken heart. Jake deserved better than someone like me. My mom had, too.

That did it. Memories of the pain on Jake's face, mingling together with images of my precious mother whose love I'd turned my back on, were more than I could take. With tears streaming down my face, I shuffled to the bathroom, grabbed the box of tissues, and shuffled back to the couch.

Covering myself in the blanket I keep there, I curled up and attempted to sob away my grief.

Chapter 25

Confiding in Max

AFTER MELODY SWATTED my declaration of love back at me like some tennis match we were playing—and she was winning—I tried my best to forget that evening ever happened and go back to the way things were before. The pain of rejection, coupled with the disappointment I felt knowing that Melody and Liam would never be the family I wanted, didn't erase my love for her. If giving her what she needed meant shoving that love, along with my own wants and desires, into some kind of emotional black hole, then so be it. That's what I would do. Because I was crazy about them both and vowed never to be any part of what was hurting either of them.

So the three of us slipped back into our previous routine. My daily agenda, mixed with trips to check on my mom and then my dad, still included visiting them every evening. Card games, books, cartoons, rounds of catch in the backyard, helping with homework— whatever Liam wanted or needed, I did it. And I kept up my goofy teasing of him, too. He still wasn't talking, but his smiles and laughter were coming more easily. So were his hugs, I noticed. He was healing, and I felt certain that a breakthrough in his persistent silence wasn't that far off.

Since neither of them was ever far from my thoughts, it came as no surprise that they were there one morning as Max and I wiped off the leg machines we'd been using.

"What's on your m-mind?" Max asked, breaking the silence between us.

"Not much," I said with a dismissive shrug. "You know, stuff like which clients I'm working with today and that sort of thing."

"R-right," he said, eyes narrowing on me. "D-don't do that. N-not with me."

"Do what? Plan my day? Do my job?"

"No—d-don't pretend n-nothing's wrong wh-when clearly s-something is b-bugging you. When are you g-going to stop t-treating me l-like I'm still your p-pesky little k-kid brother and not an actual, f-fully functioning adult? You th-think I'm too b-broken to help you or to l-listen to you? Is th-that it?"

"Shut up and don't ever say that again," I said, lightly punching him in the arm for effect. "You know that's not true."

"Then t-talk to me. Is it about L-Liam? He isn't t-talking yet?"

"He's laughing more. Smiling and showing affection more easily, so he's definitely making progress. But no, he's not talking yet."

"Okay, well, th-that's good about the p-progress. So then m-maybe it's about M-Melody?"

I nodded, giving up my ruse with a sigh. I didn't want to talk about it, really. But aside from Melody herself, Max was my only real sounding board, so why *not* tell him?

"Yeah, a few weeks ago, I, uh, kissed her. And I told her I'm falling in love with her."

"Yes!" Max crowed, his joy bringing a chuckle to my lips despite my inner turmoil. "I kn-knew it!"

"Yeah, well, don't get too excited, because she immediately friendzoned me. Shut me right down."

"What?" Considerable puzzlement wiped the triumphant glee right off his face. "I s-saw you two t-together. I'd b-bet any amount of m-money that your f-feelings are m-mutual."

"Good thing you don't have a bookie," I said. "You'd have lost that one big time."

"V-very funny, but I j-just don't believe she's t-telling you the whole s-story. Th-that doesn't m-match up with wh-what I saw that night."

"I have to take her words at face value, Maxwell. I can't be a pushy d-bag like her husband. She doesn't want me? Well, then, I guess I have to be okay with that."

"But you're *n-not* okay with it."

"Not gonna lie, it hurts," I admitted, sighing as I tossed the paper towel I'd been ripping in my hands into the trash and then leaning over to pick up my water bottle. "A lot. I want Melody and Liam to be my family. I can see the three of us together so clearly in my mind, but now that vision is painful to think about. She doesn't want it. She doesn't want *me.*"

Max grabbed his water and followed me as we went to the room I use as a makeshift office. I slid into a chair, and Max grabbed one, too.

"I'm s-sorry Jake," he said. "I was s-so lucky that L-Lily loved me b-back. I can't imagine how m-much this hurts. W-well, I *c-can* imagine it, but man it's painful to even p-picture. Th-thinking about l-losing Lily? I…I'm just s-sorry you're g-going through this."

"Thanks, man. I just have to get over it and let her go, you know? But I can't help feeling sorry for myself in the process. Like…waah, the first woman to ever truly see the real me wasn't all that interested in what she saw, you know? It makes me feel pretty bad about myself, I guess, which in turn is kind of stressing me out."

As though my stress levels were *hoping* to acknowledge the shoutout I'd just given them, a pain twisted in my chest. *I really need to call the doctor,* I told myself for the millionth time, though that notion immediately dropped from my mind as I looked up to see the alarm radiating off my brother's face. I'd thought I'd given Max a somewhat weak and watered-down explanation of what I truly was feeling, but it must have carried more weight than I imagined, because he looked downright panicky.

"Maxwell, chill out, dude," I said quickly. "You know me. I'm fine. Or at least I *will* be. Just give me time to get over her."

"I'm still w-worried about you," Max said, holding up his hand when I started to protest. "J-just shut up and l-let *me* do the w-worrying for once, okay?"

"Fine," I replied with a roll of my eyes. "But seriously, I just need to get her out of my system."

"B-by spending every s-single evening with her?"

"Yes," I said, already aware of how dumb that sounded. But I didn't want to explore any of the alternatives.

"C-can you ch-change your plans tonight or t-tomorrow?" he asked. "Have d-dinner with Lily and me? She's b-been complaining she n-never gets to s-see you. P-please?"

Not see Melody and Liam? The mere thought of an evening without them gave rise to considerable dread inside me. But then the truth of the matter was this—they weren't my family, whereas Max and Lily *were*. It was probably time for me to remember that.

"Sure," I said. "I'd like that."

Chapter 26

The Job Hunt

IT TOOK DAYS to get my nerves ready to return to the vet office where I worked all those years ago. I didn't know what to say or wear, and I definitely didn't know how to justify the way I'd walked away from them without notice or explanation.

The current employees might not remember that day, but it was on permanent display in my own mind, in big, flashing neon. It was the day I truly realized that I wasn't in a partnership with a loving spouse. Oh, sure, there had been signs long before that day, and I'd been in denial for quite some time. But that was the day I could hear the door of my prison cell close and lock. As I got in my car and drove away for the last time, it felt like I'd just been given a life sentence. All my dreams had been thrown on a bonfire so Dan could sit back and roast marshmallows in the flames that consumed them. Consumed *me*.

The other thing I wasn't sure about now was whether I needed to create an updated resumé. But what would I even put on it? I'd only ever held one job, which I had essentially abandoned. I had a high school diploma, a pile of ashes that used to be my hopes and ambitions, and a set of dubious skills. I was good at stuff like driving people away and making poor life choices.

What I wanted more than anything was to talk to Jake about it. But I also kind of felt like it was something I needed to do on my own. I knew Jake would encourage and support me; he'd probably even go with me and hold my hand if I asked. Still, I decided I needed to strap on my big-girl pants. It was time for me to stand up and wrestle a future out of the mess I'd made. That's not to say I didn't want to talk to Jake at all, but, well, maybe doing so *afterward* could be the carrot dangling on the end of my motivational stick.

In the end, I decided simply to go for it. And I chose to forget the resumé idea. I honestly wouldn't know how to create one anyway.

*   *   *

I also drove to the nail salon and had those ridiculous red nails removed. I would never risk scratching or poking an animal just for a silly show of defiance. They weren't practical, and they sure didn't reflect me as a person. They represented freedom when I first got them, but as I sat in the car staring at my bare nails instead, I was so glad the others were gone. They made me think about Dan, and that was a subject I was happy to bury, both figuratively and literally.

Finally, I drove to the clinic, parked my car, and worked to battle the nerves while scenes from my final day there continued looping and taunting me. The therapist had been giving me all kinds of suggestions for ways to battle back this type of self-doubt, so I tried to implement one—swap a bad memory for a happy memory, so I could remind myself that the good outweighs the bad. I was starting to see what she meant, because it was becoming easier to *find* good memories. Liam laughing and chasing Jake in the backyard, then wrapping himself around Jake's legs, for example. Or the devotion I saw in both their eyes when they looked at each other. And then there was Jake himself....

Even the simple act of picturing his precious face calmed me. Honestly, Jake was the best person I'd ever known. And for some reason, he liked me, too. *He even said he might be falling in love with you*, a voice in my mind reminded me. If Jake could see something worth loving inside me, then that thing might actually exist. So I was going to be okay, no matter what else happened today, because I had Jake in my life. If I didn't know anything else, I knew that.

With Jake still on my mind, I released the seatbelt, grabbed my key fob and shoved it in my purse, and climbed out of the car. I could do this.

When I walked inside, I didn't know whether to be disappointed or relieved when none of the faces behind the receptionist's desk looked familiar.

"Hi," a blonde with a high ponytail said to me. "What's the name of your pet?"

"Oh, uh, no pet," I said, my palms sweating now. "I, uh, used to work here. Years ago. Is Julie still the office manager? The one who does the hiring?"

"Julie Tamsen? Yeah, hang on."

She disappeared, heading in the direction of Julie's old office—apparently some things *hadn't* changed—and soon returned with a wave of her hand beckoning me to join her.

"Honestly, I don't think we're hiring," she told me, her demeanor still warm and welcoming, "but Julie was curious who the returning employee might be."

"Thanks. I appreciate your help."

"No problem." She gestured toward Julie's open door. "Here you go!"

I gave her a weak wave, took a deep breath, and walked in.

*   *   *

"Melody!" Julie said, shocking me by standing up, circling her desk, and pulling me into a hug. "I'd hoped it was you!"

"You…you…did?" I said, spluttering my confusion at her. "I have to be honest, after the way I left, I figured there was a huge likelihood that I wasn't going to be particularly welcome around here."

"Have a seat honey," she said. "And of course you're welcome here."

"Thank you." I dug around in my purse for a tissue, but there weren't any. "I came hoping there might be an opening. I really want my job back. I…I want you to know that I never wanted to leave it in the first place."

"I kind of thought there was something else going on that day," Julie said, reaching behind her desk to grab a box of her own tissues and sliding them toward me. "What happened, if you don't mind me asking?"

"I don't mind telling you," I said immediately. "I owe you that much at the very least. The thing was, I was married to…well, a really controlling man. He cut me off one by one from my family and friends. Then he made me quit this job I loved. By doing that, he was also making me abandon my dream of becoming a veterinarian. For my part, well…I *let* him do those things. So I'm not exactly an innocent bystander here."

"No," she said, shaking her head, which caused my stomach to plummet. "Don't do that. Don't victim-blame yourself. Did he lay out his plans to break you down and dominate you before you married him?"

"No, of course not."

"Then you simply had the misfortune of believing in the false front he put up in order to get you," she said. "You were such a wonderful employee, such a natural with all the animals. Even the scared or defiant ones. It always nagged at me, the way you left. I…well, I can't tell you how happy I am to see you again."

"Thank you," I said. "I never would have left in the manner that I did if I'd had a choice."

"So I take it things are better now?" she asked. "Divorced him, huh?"

"Actually, a drunk driver did me a bit of a favor," I said, wincing at how that sounded. "I'm sorry. I know that's harsh. Let's just say I'm a widow who may have skipped straight to the acceptance stage of the grief process."

"I'll bet you did," she said, a wry smile on her face. "Now, about a job…."

Chapter 27

Happy News and Sad Truths

I WAS BURSTING with the need to tell Jake about my day, and I all but tackled him when he walked through the door that evening.

"Hey Melo—" he started to say, then emitted a funny *Oomph!* when I bounced into his arms like a human superball.

"I got my old job back!" I squealed, and probably a bit too loudly considering my face was burrowed in his neck. "I did it!"

Most of his laughs came out as lazy chuckles, so the delighted whoop of true, rolling laughter that my news elicited from him only ratcheted up my joy. If we'd been gaming, I'd say his laughter served to unlock the next level on my happiness game.

"Okay, woman," he said after I peeled myself off him. "Let's sit down while you back up this train. What job? Where? What's going on with you, and why didn't you tell me about it sooner?"

Without even thinking about smart topics like fuzzy boundaries or mixed signals, I gleefully laced my fingers through his and tugged him over to the couch. Meanwhile, Liam intercepted Jake halfway across the living room in his own version of a bear hug. If nothing else, Jake certainly had to be feeling very welcome in our home, I thought idly as I plopped down and tugged him to my side.

"Liam, your mama has some happy news she

wants to share with me," Jake said. "Why don't you give us a few minutes for some adult talk. Can you read a few books in your room for a little while? I promise we'll play later, okay, buddy?"

Liam looked disappointed but simply nodded at Jake, smiled at me, and walked away.

"Okay," Jake said, turning his focus on me again, "I'm dying here, so tell me this news of yours."

"I, um...." I began hesitantly, a little unsure how much detail to give. Without the full context, though, my news wouldn't really match my zinging levels of glee. So I decided to just plunge into the whole thing. "I don't want to bring myself down, but this story starts sad."

"Hey, just tell me what you *want* to tell me, okay?" he said. "Not pushing you here."

"I know. But there's a lot you don't know about me, which means there's a lot I *want* you to know. So, of course, I'm leaving out a billion details, but, well, here it is—I grew up loving animals, but we were 'can't even afford a double-wide' kind of poor, you know what I mean?"

"Yeah."

"It was just my mom and me. Never knew my dad. She had to work loads of hours and leave me to latchkey myself through my childhood. She was the best mom ever, but that's as much as she could do."

He nodded. "I get it. She sounds like another strong mama I know."

"Crap, you're going to get me crying already," I replied, reaching for the box of tissues I'd never gotten around to taking back out of the living room. "But yeah, she was so strong. Anyway, we obviously couldn't afford pets. She could barely afford *me*. But she nurtured my love of animals regardless, and she encouraged my dreams of becoming a veterinarian one day."

"I had no idea you even liked animals," Jake said. "That's a great dream, Mel."

"Was," I corrected. "It *was* a great dream. I'm sure you can infer everything I'm not saying, but Dan didn't support it, and I never ended up taking even a single college course. I did work for a while in a vet clinic as a tech, however, and I absolutely loved everything about it."

"Is that where you went today?"

"It is," I said, my smile creeping back out from behind the tears that were falling because of the memories of my mom. "They didn't even have any openings, but they made one for me after I explained why I'd quit with no notice all those years ago."

Jake was now lightly tracing circles on my hand with his thumb. "Dan cutting you off from everything you loved, I suppose?"

"Of course," I said.

Then he stopped his lazy circles to look back up at me in shock. "You removed the nails!"

"Yeah, it was time. Can't be accidentally stabbing someone's sweet, unsuspecting doggo."

"No, that wouldn't be a good idea. Okay, so, I have another question. But I'm afraid it'll bring even more tears to your eyes."

"Go ahead. I seem to cry at everything lately anyway."

"Where's your mom now? You've never mentioned your family before."

He was right—the tears came even faster. "Wow you weren't kidding."

"Sorry, Mel," he said. "Don't answer that. Forget I asked."

"No, I don't want to keep secrets from you. It's just that this subject is my biggest shame. My mom put me first her whole life, but Dan didn't like her. He was embarrassed by her. She was poor and low-class, at least in his eyes, so he didn't want her around us, especially once the baby came along. For the longest time, I'd just go see her on my own. But the more he took away my freedoms—including my car, eventually—the harder it was to spend time with her. She tried coming here, but it was always such a scene that it was easier just to make up excuses to avoid her visits, you know?"

Jake didn't say anything, but his tightened squeeze on my hand gave me the courage to keep going with the story.

"When Liam was born, she wanted to come see him, of course. Dan wouldn't leave me alone long enough to have her see me at the hospital, although she did get to see Liam—well, viewed him through the glass at the nursery. But at least she got to *see* him. Thank God. That thought was all that kept me going in the days after I found out she died soon after. She had cancer, and she was never able to tell me. She probably thought I wouldn't have even cared."

"I can't imagine that's true," Jake said gently. "Did she know anything about Dan's true nature? Had you ever confided in her?"

"No, I never told her what was going on. But, well...she saw his anger for herself a few times, and she heard some of his nastier cutting remarks."

"Mel, she knew exactly what was going on with you," Jake said. "That's precisely why she wasn't showing up in your hospital room and screaming about her rights as the grandmother. Think about it. *Really* think about it. What does a mother do in that situation, a mother who adores her baby girl and only wants to keep her safe from her abuser? She stays away, that's what. She avoids making it worse for you. It's as clear as a Times Square billboard to me, honey. She absolutely knew that you loved her but were in an impossible situation, and she loved you so much that she did anything she could to keep from escalating the pain or danger. You didn't just confess a horribly dark mistake; you told me a beautiful love story."

"Only you could make me feel better after I told that story for the first time," I replied, my tears now like a faucet set on full blast. His gentle words of reassurance had somehow managed to chisel off a small chunk of the self-loathing I'd been lugging around in my personal baggage since my mom died. I'd never thought about it that way before—that maybe she knew and simply loved me too much to get Dan riled up by shoving herself into our drama. I knew I'd be replaying Jake's words in my next therapy session, too. I'd never dared to talk about my mom with the therapist yet, but it seemed like it might finally be time.

"Let's celebrate tomorrow," I said, trying to inject some of my previous joy into our conversation again. "I got my job back, and you're the only person, besides Liam, who I want to share my happiness with."

"Yes, I definitely want to celebrate with both of you," he said, "but it can't be tomorrow. I've got a family dinner to go to."

"Right, okay, no worries, we can do it another time," I said, even as regret wrapped itself around me like a clenched fist.

Jake was going to spend time with his family. And that family could never include me.

Chapter 28

The Family Dinner

"WOW, IT'S SO GOOD to see you!" Lily squealed, wrapping me inside a sweetly enthusiastic hug. "Where've you been?!"

"Same old, same old, Lils," I said, squeezing her in return before she finally untangled herself and drew back to look me over. "You know me," I went on, "all work and no play."

"You…are you feeling okay?" she asked, a cute little furrow of worry lines emerging on her forehead. "There's something off about you. Maybe it's your coloring? You don't look like the healthy guy I met that day in the lobby of my apartment."

"L-let's at least g-go inside and get a t-table before we pick J-Jake apart," Max suggested, wrapping his arm around Lily. The way he touched her was both gentle and sweet.

"Good idea as always, Maxwell," I said, trying to sound chipper despite the inner worry that Lily's concern had fueled. She was right, after all: I *didn't* feel well. Hadn't for a while, if I was being completely honest with myself. I'd been ignoring the signs and symptoms for a long time now, and I probably would for a while more. I just didn't have the time to deal with it. I couldn't get off the treadmill I'd been on since dad's accident. Then again, I knew I'd been running on it long *before* the day of that accident. That day simply caused me to turn up the speed. *Maybe that's all that's wrong with me,* I thought as we walked toward the entrance of the restaurant. *Maybe I'm simply exhausted.*

Once we were seated, Lily tried again.

"Seriously, is everything okay with you? I know you're friends now with a lady named Melody. Max told me all about you meeting her and her son. And he told me he suspects you and Melody have feelings for each other. Is that what's wrong? Heartache?"

"L-Lily!" Max said, laughter in his voice. "Ease up on the g-guy!"

"You didn't tell her?" I asked Max. "I figured talking to you was the same as advertising on the Tell-a-Lily Hotline."

"N-not my story to t-tell," Max replied, shrugging behind his menu. "I don't b-break confidences."

"Tell me what?" Lily asked. "Or wait, no—forget I said that. Max is right. If you're confiding in him, then it's none of my business. I'm sorry. I'm seriously not trying to be nosy. I just care about you, and I wasn't lying that you don't look like you're feeling well to me. But if you say you're fine, then I'll drop it. Say, that's some interesting weather we've been having, huh?"

Max and I both chuckled at her game, and slightly lame, attempt at changing the subject.

"To be fair," I said, "I haven't been able to say much at all. Can't get a word in edgewise with you two."

"Ugh!" Lily replied. "I'm sorry. You know how I can get. I've already got an entire love story about you and Melody written in my head."

"Well, good," I told her with a nod. "And I hope we end up together in your story, but it doesn't look like we will in real life. That's what I was talking about with Max. I told her I'm falling for her, and she immediately stabbed me in the chest with a friendzone designation."

Lily's eyes widened. "No! I *hate* the friendzone! I used to live there, after all. But what's wrong with her, anyway? There's no woman alive who wouldn't be madly in love with you, Jake!"

"I c-can hear you, you kn-know," Max said, still behind his menu. "I'm s-sitting right here."

"And you know I'm the one exception, my love," Lily said, batting her eyelids and pressing a kiss to his cheek before turning back to me. "But seriously, she's lying."

I shrugged. "I appreciate the support and the vote of confidence, but if she says it, then I have to accept it. She's a widow. Her husband was a total nozzle, and she's got all kinds of issues related to that. So does Liam."

"Oh, I'm so sorry to hear it," Lily said, wilting like the flower she was named for. I love Lily because she's so good for my brother, of course. But her innate kindness and empathy are incredible. I'd love her like a sister in pretty much any context. "That breaks my heart. Is there anything Max and I can do to help?"

"Max talked to Liam already, as you know. So, yeah, he did his part. But otherwise, no, I think they both just need time. Y'know, to heal."

"That makes sense."

The conversation paused when the server approached and asked for our orders. I'd been so busy talking that I hadn't looked at the menu. I needed to find something bland that wouldn't clamp my stomach in a vise, even though basically everything I ate had that effect on me lately. I settled on soup and a salad, no dressing, and ignored the worried look that Lily shot at Max.

As they placed their own orders, I thought about what Lily had suggested. Part of me would love to bring us all together. Melody and Liam would probably both adore her, and it would be good for Melody to have a female friend. The sad part, though, was that I don't think that would be good for *me*. I wanted Melody and Liam to be my family so badly that I already felt like I could almost reach out and touch that vision. But I couldn't; it was just that—a vision in my mind and nothing more. Combining them with my actual family would only make it hurt more.

Once the server left, Max leaned forward, trapping me in a steely gaze.

"I've b-been thinking about wh-what you said," he started. "Y'know, about how Melody shut you down. I th-think you're right that she j-just needs time."

"And that's what I plan to give her," I assured him. "I don't want to pressure her. My friendship is hers whether she loves me back or not."

"That's g-good. I was the M-Melody in my own love story, r-remember. Even th-though I was absolutely c-crazy about L-Lily, I w-wasn't ready. We were just f-friends for a long t-time, until I f-finally felt I could be the p-partner she deserves."

"I hear what you're saying," I told him, hope now fluttering around in my chest. "You think she may well love me already, but this isn't our time yet."

"Exactly," he said, nodding, as Lily leaned over to give him another kiss on the cheek. He spotted this and turned, gentle smiles on both their faces as he captured the kiss on his lips instead.

Yeah, I wanted what they had. Desperately. Melody had told me that we could never be more than friends, but maybe that wasn't the whole truth. Maybe she was scared or didn't want me putting my life on hold while she took the time she needed. But that's where she wasn't getting it.

I'd wait for her—forever, if necessary.

Chapter 29

The Good News

AFTER WE SAID our goodbyes, I was all wound up, my feelings for Melody bursting and popping like fireworks in the air around me. The idea Max had planted—the one that said Melody loved me back, but it just wasn't our time yet—had already taken root inside my chest. I wanted to believe it so badly that it hurt.

Also, I missed her and Liam. I hadn't spent an evening apart from them in months. I hated that I didn't yet know how Liam did on his math test or what Melody might have learned today when she went into the clinic. Her plan had been to update her employee record and then get an idea of what had changed in the years since she left.

I glanced at my phone. It was too late to see Liam; he was sure to be asleep. But Melody would still be up, likely reading on the couch or scrolling through her messages. I hesitated a moment, my thumbs poised over my own phone. Would saying hi be too pushy? I wasn't sure. But I couldn't stop thinking about her. In the end, I decided a text wouldn't hurt, so I tried to keep it light.

Me: How'd it go at the clinic?

She must have been right where I was picturing her—in the living room, phone in her hand—because her reply was almost instantaneous.

Melody: Hey, it was great! Mostly all new faces, but

everyone was so nice. How was dinner?

Me: Good. Those two are so cute. But I spent the whole night trying to convince Lily I'm not sick, lol.

Melody: What? You're sick?):

Me: Nah, she just likes to fuss over everyone. Missed you guys tonight!

Melody: We missed you, too! Liam was so dejected when I told him it would just be the two of us tonight. I was almost offended, lol.

Me: I'll make it up to him tomorrow.

Melody: Tired? Heading to bed?

Me: Nah, I'm wired. Still sitting in my truck outside the restaurant. Had to check in first.

Melody: Why don't you swing by and tell me about your day? I'm up and wired, too. Plus, I've got some good news.

My heart started pounding at her invitation, swept away in a tidal wave of hope. Maybe Max *was* right. Maybe the love was already there, and she simply needed time before she could embrace it.

I shot back a quick text, confirming I was on my way.

*　　*　　*

I sent another text the moment I got there, afraid to wake Liam with a knock.

"Hey," she said, opening the door and gesturing for me to enter. "I'm happy you decided to swing by."

When we entered the living room, I hesitated. Should I sit alone in the recliner, ensuring that I wouldn't be pushing her boundaries? Was sitting side-by-side on the couch late at night too intimate, given where we were in our relationship? I didn't want to push her. But then, just as I was deciding the recliner was the safer choice, she grabbed my arm and tugged me with her toward the couch.

"Plop down and relax a minute," she said. "Need anything to drink before I do the same?"

"Nope," I said. This effort for me to join her on the couch further fanned the flames of hope in my chest. "I'm good."

She sat down then at the other end, tucking her feet underneath her before unleashing a sunny smile on her beautiful face.

"So, tell me about your good news," I said, breaking the somewhat awkward silence that had settled between us. "What's behind that smile? You look so happy, Mel, which is making *me* happy."

"I just had the best day," she replied. "Get this: Julie and the head vet, Dr. Kim—he's the owner—sat me down and talked to me. He asked me a bunch of questions about my background with animals and my plans for my future. I was really open and frank with them both about what had happened with Dan. I said that being a vet tech would be more than I could ever hope for at this point, and I'm so grateful for the opportunity. Guess what they said to that?"

"I'm a terrible guesser; ask Liam," I said with a chuckle. I'd never seen her so light and optimistic before. It was a glorious sight to behold—and if I had any say in it at all, it would soon become her default setting. "What'd they say?"

"They said that if I want to start taking college classes, they'll offer tuition reimbursement!" She all but shrieked this. "In exchange, I'd promise to work for a set number of years as a vet in that clinic once I graduated. As though I'd ever leave!"

"Are you serious right now? Mel, I am *so* happy for you! You deserve this, honey."

"Thank you!" she said, happy tears glistening in her eyes. "I just can't believe it yet. I've been floating around in shock ever since that meeting."

"I take it you said yes?"

"Of course! Although I did also tell them about Liam's situation. I can't go full-time right away. Seeing him through this trauma and getting both of us to our therapy appointments has to remain my primary focus. It'll be years before I could possibly graduate and make good on that promise to them."

"No biggie," I said. "You're young."

She sighed. "Yeah, I am. It's just…it's more than I ever could have hoped for, you know? I'm so happy, but part of me just doesn't feel like I deserve it. And I wish I could tell my mom, and that also makes me sad, as you know. It's just…a lot of warring emotions."

"I get that," I told her. "But you *do* deserve all the happiness in the world, Mel. You do. And I'll bet your mom is up there in heaven smiling like crazy and so happy for her baby girl."

"You always know exactly the right thing to say," she said, wiping away a tear. "Can I get a hug?"

"Of course," I said, opening my arms wide toward her as she unfolded herself. With a shy smile, she climbed over and right into my arms.

I closed my eyes and held on tight, wishing with everything inside me that I didn't eventually have to let go.

Chapter 30

The Kiss

BEING IN HIS ARMS felt like the safest place in the world. It was like everything I'd gone through in my life had simply been a set of necessary steps to wind up right there, tucked inside his muscular arms and with my cheek pressed against his broad chest as I listened to the steady thump of his heart. He felt like my true north, and I would have given anything in that moment to hold on tight and never let go.

So when he leaned down to press a soft kiss on my cheek, I wasn't thinking about all the reasons I'd given that we could only be friends. I was thinking instead about his warm and strong embrace. How good he smelled. And how happy, safe, and content I always felt when I was with him. Those thoughts made me lift my head off his chest, stare deep into his brown eyes, and then lean forward to kiss him.

I wasn't prepared for the jolt of electricity that short-circuited my brain the moment our lips came together. Even when we were young and hormonal and totally in love, kissing Dan had never, not once, felt as good to me as that passion-fueled kiss felt with Jake. As we tasted and tested and explored, my heart felt so full that I almost didn't know how to process it. Nothing in my life had ever felt so satisfying and right.

So maybe it was an outlier. Maybe it wasn't something that really *should* be in my life.

With that thought, I suddenly realized what I was

doing: I was sending Jake mixed signals. Nothing had changed, and we still couldn't be together. So I had absolutely no right to be kissing him like this. No right at all.

I gasped and pulled back from his embrace, almost crab-walking back to my end of the sofa. My chest was heaving as I attempted to pull enough oxygen into my lungs. He'd left me feeling weak, stunned, and breathless.

"Mel, honey, what's wrong?" he asked, his words slow and deliberate, like he was trying to tame a wild horse. "I thought we were really connecting there, and I've never been so happy before. But…why do you look so miserable suddenly? You're scaring me."

"We shouldn't have done that," I said. "I know that it was my fault. I kissed you. But…it doesn't change things between us."

"It kind of feels like it does, though," he replied, confusion and misery battling on his face. "I don't know about you, but I have never been so blown away by something as simple as a kiss before. That was incredible, Mel. *We* are incredible together. Tell me you felt it, too. You *must* have."

Feel it? Of course I felt it. It was like he just finished rewiring all the synapses in my body, leaving me sort of shaky and off-kilter.

"No," I said, knowing I'd never be able to make him really understand. "We're just friends, Jake. I told you that. We can only ever just be friends."

"I'm sorry," he said. "I don't think I'm ever going to be able to give up hoping for more. I thought I was falling for you before, but after that kiss? I'm already there."

"Don't you dare waste your life waiting on me," I

said, suddenly realizing that I had to set him free. I loved him way too much to let him lose opportunities to find a partner who wasn't totally broken, the way I was. A partner who could trust her instincts enough to return that love fully, the way he deserved to be loved. But in order to set him free, I was going to have to be cruel. Otherwise, he wasn't going to accept it.

"None of the time I've spent with you was a waste," he said. "And let me worry about how I spend my life."

"Jake, here's the thing," I said, pausing to brace myself. It was going to be the worst kind of torture to watch the painful effects of the words I was about to unleash on this amazing man. "I told you I couldn't ever be with another controlling man. No way. Not after the things Dan did to me."

"*Of course* you shouldn't be with a controlling man," he countered. "But I'm not Dan. I could *never* be like him. I would never try to tell you what to do or how to live your life. I'll say it again: that's not me. I'm not controlling."

"Yes you are," I fired back, my words ringing with conviction. I was startled at my acting ability as I continued twisting the knife. "You're controlling every single person in your family, even as we speak."

"What are you talking about? Where is this coming from, Mel?"

"You haven't told either of your brothers about your dad, have you? And it's not looking like you ever intend to, either. Mitch doesn't deserve the chance to confront his feelings about his father while the man's still breathing? Max—sweet, kind Max—doesn't get the opportunity to face his abuser, either? And why? Because *you* say so? Who died and made you the emotional gatekeeper? Oh yeah, Dan did. And your dad might, too. But you're the only one who gets the chance to make peace with it, huh?"

Jake's mouth fell open, the shock seeming to paralyze him so much that his reaction to my words was delayed. I was still gasping for air; the energy it had taken to force myself to say those horrible things to him was roughly equal to running a marathon. I felt dirty and cruel and wretched. But I'd said those things because I loved him. They were cruel, yes, but *necessary*. I had to set him free.

I watched in silence as Jake started rubbing his chest. He looked sort of pale and sweaty, and I worried that I'd gone too far.

"Are you okay?" I asked.

That seemed to startle him, and he suddenly lurched to his feet.

"Jake?" I asked again, standing now, too. "You don't look well. I…I'm sorry for what I said. Let me get you some water or something."

"No," he said kind of quietly. "Don't. I was just leaving."

Tears returned to my eyes. "Jake, I'm sorry. I didn't want to hurt you. I just want us to be friends."

"We…we aren't friends," he said, stepping back as I attempted to approach him.

"Yes!" I cried in response. "Jake, we're *best* friends! But I need you to understand I can't give you anything more!"

"Tell Liam I love him very much," he said, his hand still pressed to his chest as he turned toward the door. He pulled it open, then turned back to face me once again. "And Melody?"

"Yes?" I asked, breathlessly hoping he was going to say he forgave me.

"I'm sorry for not being the man you needed me to be."

Chapter 31

The Fog

SOMETHING WAS WRONG. Really, really wrong.

Yes, I knew full well that I'd been ignoring the signs and symptoms for months now. I'd brushed off Lily's concern when she spotted me earlier and immediately noticed my coloring was weird. But then Melody also said I didn't look well. She may not want to have me in her life as a partner, but after that night I could never again doubt that she totally knew me. Melody could see inside to places *I* never even went. So if she said I didn't look well, then I really didn't.

She'd nailed it with her assessment of me, after all. It turns out that I'm every bit as controlling as Dan ever was. Her words hit me like a lightning bolt because she was *right*. I'd been so busy trying to justify my actions simply as part of my big-brother duties. That's what I do, right? I care for Max. It's always been like I was holding down two full-time jobs, and protecting him was one of them.

But Melody was right that this type of protection wasn't the same thing as love. Blocking his ability to stand at our father's bedside while listing off alphabetically the many ways the old man had failed as a father or simply to forgive him? That was just cruel. Max deserved that chance, and I was the only thing standing in his way. Our father had to be larger than life in his mind, almost the proverbial monster under his bed. But if Max had even two seconds to stand at our father's bedside and see how weak, pitiful, and withered he was, maybe my father's grip on his psyche would lessen. And I was the human roadblock preventing that from happening.

So her words gave me some much-needed clarity that night, plus a huge shock to my system. And it was that jolt of understanding that seemed to be the last nail in the coffin where my health crisis was concerned. As I sat there with her words fully soaking into my brain and rewiring my nerve endings, I became fairly convinced that I was having a heart attack. And not a "lovesick revelation that Melody seriously wanted nothing to do with me" type of heart attack, although I was having that, too. No, I mean that *literally*. I felt like I was having *some* type of cardiac event.

The last thing I wanted to do was traumatize Melody further. She didn't need to stand there while EMTs flopped me around on a gurney like the catch of the day. And what if Liam had gotten up and ended up witnessing that? No, no way.

So I'd scrambled out to my truck as quickly as I could move, strapped on the seatbelt, and headed for the emergency room.

*   *   *

Her words were still looping through my brain as I drove, and I forced myself to feel the pain over and over in the hopes that the brittle edges would poke through the fog that was circling me. That fog was aggressively moving closer and threatening to pull me under; my hands were in a white-knuckled clench on the steering wheel as I fought to stay upright and conscious.

Feel the pain.... Focus on the pain....

That was my game plan as I made my way across town toward the emergency room, but of course I was hitting every red light and getting stuck behind every meandering driver.

So yeah, the pain....

I needed to focus on it. It was, of course, *way* too easy to access. I had a feeling that Melody's rejection of me and my stupid domineering attempts at love would leave me bleeding for a very long time. If I survived that night, that is.

I'd found my soulmate; I knew that much as fact. But I was too much of a controlling mess for her to ever trust me or love me back. She'd pretty much have to punch me in the face with the truth in order for me to see it. She and I weren't going to end up together. We weren't going to be a family. Liam would never be my son.

I suppose I could find a way to blame this on my dad. And honestly, the mental gymnastics of getting to that point wouldn't be all that strenuous. I mean, really, if I hadn't been forced to assume the role of Max's father from my early teens, maybe I wouldn't have turned into this professional protector. Maybe I'd have a life of my own. Maybe I'd stop turning down invites to hang out with Tyrone and the other guys at the gym.

And maybe Melody would love me back.

But as easy as it would be to blame my father—I mean really, what's one more log in the enormous bonfire that had been fueled by his sins and misdeeds?—it would be childish for me to try to blame someone else. I alone had made the decision to keep Max in the dark about our dear old dad. And I alone had done the same thing to Mitch. Mitch might not be as much of a victim of our father's brutality as Max was, but he certainly hadn't emerged from his childhood unscathed, either. The fact that he was still hiding from all of us across the country was proof enough: He surely bore emotional scars just as we did. But I was holding back on letting him make peace with those feelings, too. And just because I didn't want to feel the sting of his rejection again? How had I managed to make all of this about me anyway?

Another ache shot through my chest, and I struggled to breathe through the pain and remain conscious, even as the driver in the next lane cut right in front of me. I slammed on the brakes and yanked my steering wheel, causing my truck to lurch and shake wildly as I fought to regain control. I won the battle somehow, and I was able to cruise to a stop on the side of the road. I sat there a moment to catch my breath, but the jolt of adrenaline I'd just gotten was more than my body could handle.

The fog started creeping toward me again, and then it devoured me.

Chapter 32

The Unknown Caller

I WAS GUTTED. The look on Jake's face when he walked out my door—probably for the last time—and the words he'd said to me had ripped me open as surely as if he'd been holding a knife at the time.

I'm sorry for not being the man you needed me to be.

He was sorry?! *I'm* the one who was broken and unworthy. I'm the one who'd married and stayed with a horrible man. I'm the one who brought a child into this world with that man, knowing the whole time that man would likely be a terrible father. I'm the one who turned away from my own mother. And I'm the one who, when offered the heart and love of the kindest and most generous person on the planet, threw it back in his face. And as the topper on all those mistakes, I'd somehow also managed to make him feel like *he* was the villain in our tale rather than who he really was: the handsome prince.

I tried to comfort myself with the knowledge that I'd accomplished what I had set out to do: I'd driven him away and set him free. He'd no longer carry around the false hope that we could ever be together, and he wouldn't ever get chained to the miserable fate of waiting and wishing for me to become a worthy partner for him.

Liam was my top priority anyway, and he had to remain so. I'd done this for him. I couldn't trust my baby with any man, not even one as wonderful as Jake.

That was the lesson Dan had drilled into me, right?

Convincing myself again and again that I'd done the right thing for Liam wasn't easy, and Liam himself was part of the reason why. He was just so mopey and forlorn all morning as we tried to move through the steps of our routine to get him ready for school. He was moving slowly, and we barely made it to the car in time.

"Aren't you feeling well, buddy?" I asked him, looking to see his reactions in my rearview mirror as I drove. When he shrugged, I carried on with, "Didn't you sleep very well?"

He gave a small shake of his head to indicate he hadn't.

"Are you worried about something at school?" Again the shake—*no*. "Are you upset with something I did?" *No....*

I was avoiding asking him about Jake, but it was becoming apparent that Jake's absence the night before was the cause of his unhappiness. And now, thanks to me, there was a huge chance that Jake wouldn't be back that evening, either. Or the following night. Or the night after that. Or *any* night in the future. In trying to protect Liam by setting Jake free, I might have destroyed both the boy and the man. Regret twisted angrily inside me as I took a deep breath and asked the obvious question.

"Honey, are you upset because Jake didn't come over last night?" I asked, holding my breath even as he immediately met my eyes in the mirror and nodded an emphatic yes. "Oh honey, I'm sorry. Jake was spending some time with his own family. You remember his brother Max, right? Max and his girlfriend Lily wanted to see Jake. They love him every bit as much as we, uh, *you* do. We've been hogging all his time away from them. It was just their turn, that's all. Oh, and actually Jake asked me to tell you he loves you very much, okay sweetheart?"

I pulled up to the line of cars, each queued for a turn to unload their little students into the waiting arms of the staff who greeted them each morning. When we got up there, I watched as he unbuckled his car seat and grabbed his backpack.

"I love you, buddy," I said as he slid out of the door and stopped to wave at me. I could see a sad little smile on his face just before he closed the door and turned to join the other kids walking toward the main entrance. I waved back even though he'd already turned around, then I attempted to force my attention back to the task of driving and my main errand ahead of me that day.

In the years since I'd last been employed at the clinic, the workers had been asked to start wearing scrubs. Julie said it was because vet techs were routinely splattered with all kinds of filth that no sane person would want on their street clothes. But Dr. Kim also liked the look of professionalism that scrubs provided. So my task was to find and purchase several sets of blue scrubs, along with sneakers or other comfortable shoes for long days of being on my feet.

This largely mindless task was a welcome relief from what I'd otherwise be doing all day: paddling around in an ocean of regret. The look on Jake's face, coupled with his haunting last words, were still right there in my mind. Shopping at least served as a way to shove them off the main stage for a while.

By the time I got home with my purchases, I'd almost managed to convince myself that I might be able to survive without him. That's when my phone lit up with a call from an unknown number. It was local, so I wondered if it might be someone at Liam's school. That's the only reason I tapped the green button to accept it.

"Hello?" I said, hoping I hadn't just connected with a telemarketer.

"Hi, is this Melody?" an unfamiliar voice asked. "Jake's Melody?"

"I'm…what?" I said, thrown off by the designation. "Um, yes, this is Melody. And yes, I know Jake."

"This is Lily," she said. Only then did I realize that she was crying. "Max's girlfriend?"

"Yes, of course I know who you are," I said, frantic now. "What's wrong, Lily?"

"We don't know yet, exactly," she said. "All we know is that Jake's in the hospital, and that…oh Melody, I think it's really bad."

I gasped as icy dread clutched my heart. *No!!!*

She told me which hospital to go to and how to find them when I arrived. Then she gave me a series of phone numbers—hers, Max's, Mitch's, and that of someone named Claire. I didn't even question this; I just programmed them into my phone. Then I called Celeste and asked if she and Ron would mind picking up Liam and keeping him overnight. No surprise, but she was thrilled, assuring me that he'd do his homework and have a fun evening with them. They were on my list of people who had my permission to pick up Liam from school, but I dropped an email to his teacher anyway, alerting her about the change of plans.

These tasks prevented me from panicking, which is what I really wanted to do. Jake hadn't looked well the previous night, but I'd purposely hurt him anyway and then stood back and let him leave. What had happened after he drove away from me? And how much of it was my fault? I didn't know the answers to any of these questions, but there was something I did know, and I knew it with a fierce conviction—losing Dan had barely been a ripple in the waters of my life. But if Jake died? No…I could barely even stand to let that question form in my mind.

If Jake died, I'd never recover.

Chapter 33

The Waiting Room

I DON'T REMEMBER the drive to the hospital. I'd gone from helplessly standing in my kitchen as Lily's horrific news drove spears into my chest to once again walking through the halls of that blasted hospital.

Yes, it was the very same hospital where I'd fearfully but resolutely—was it really just a few months ago?—searched for the room of the man who'd killed Dan. I'd been overwhelmed that day. And scared. And alone. But those emotions couldn't even begin to compare to the avalanche of fear and worry and panic that were beating a punishing rhythm inside my chest as I looked for Max and Lily.

When I found them, Max immediately stood while our gazes connected. We approached each other, a hesitant awkwardness coiling its way around us. I knew Max's history, of course, so I understood why he wasn't sure if he should hug me, wave, or bolt from the room. For my part, hugging wasn't exactly my go-to move, thanks to Dan. He'd made it *very* clear that I wasn't to touch other men, even in harmless social interactions. So, in the end, we both sort of shuffled up to each other and halted, our fears bouncing and reflecting off each other.

"Hi Melody, I'm Lily," Max's companion said as she approached cautiously. "I'm so sorry we're meeting like this. Can I give you a hug?"

I could probably count the number of hugs I'd

received from other women on one hand, especially since my mother died, so I gratefully accepted hers. She smelled like coconut and vanilla, and I felt soothed by her presence.

"What happened?" I asked as we finally drew back from each other. Her beautiful blue eyes were red-rimmed and puffy, which meant she'd shed a lot of tears. My worries ratcheted even higher as I wondered what the two of them were about to tell me.

"L-let's sit," Max said, and I joined them in the corner of the waiting room where I'd found them. "We d-don't know m-much, though. L-Lily? C-can you…I j-just c-can't…."

"Of course," she said, pausing to lean over and press a kiss to his lips before turning to me. "Jake passed out in his truck on the side of a street. He'd managed to put it in park, but the car was running. I guess a passerby called 9-1-1."

"This was this morning?"

"No, they found him last night," Lily told me as dread clenched tightly in my chest. *Last night?* He left my house last night…and then passed out? My heart started racing as guilt and panic stirred up a toxic brew inside of me. "Here's where it gets confusing, though," she went on. "The doctors did all kinds of tests on him, but pretty much everything was negative. I mean, we all know how well Jake takes care of himself. It wasn't a stroke. It wasn't a heart attack. It wasn't a seizure. He tested negative for drugs or alcohol. Although they did say something about his gallbladder. Oh, and they asked us about his stress levels, but we don't know of any cause he might have for being stressed. The doctor wants to talk to you about that, though. He seems to really be focusing on stress for some reason."

Yeah–it was my fault. I'd stressed Jake out so badly that he'd had some sort of medical episode. To be fair, Jake's stress levels were high before I ever opened my stupid mouth that night...but Max and Lily didn't know about any of that.

"Me?" I asked. "The doctor wants to talk to *me?*"

Lily nodded. "Yeah, he asked who else might have insight into Jake's life, so of course we mentioned you. Oh, wait...actually, he said you should go to the nurse's desk and have him paged when you got here. It's Dr. Aquino."

"Okay, uh, I'll go do that," I said, jerkily rising to my feet. "I'll be right back."

*   *   *

I waited at the nurse's station, grateful to have a little space away from Max and Lily. As much as I believed Max needed to know about his father, I certainly wasn't going to be the one to tell him.

"Ms. Harper?" someone asked, shaking me out of my cloud of worry. I turned to see a very slight man briskly moving toward me, his dark eyes boring into me as he made his quick approach. "I'm Dr. Aquino."

"Please call me Melody," I replied. "I'm Jake Cruz's...uh, friend."

With a quick nod and no smile, he said, "Nice to meet you. So, what can you tell me about his stress levels?"

"They're sky high, something he's been actively trying to shelter his brother from, as you've probably figured out. Why? What's going on?"

"He's an incredibly fit, mostly otherwise healthy young man, with the blood pressure of an obese, chain-smoking retiree. When the EMTs brought him in, his blood pressure was dangerously elevated, and we haven't been able to bring it down much. We're keeping him sedated now because he seems to get upset each time he wakes up. So, okay…what do you know that his brother doesn't?"

I sighed. "A lot of things. His dad is in a coma right here in this hospital. He's in Room 612, in case you need any family history or genetic information. Mitchell Cruz is his name. He was very abusive to Max, the brother you spoke with, so Jake's been hiding the dad's coma and dealing with all the ramifications alone."

"I see," he said, jotting down some notes. "Anything else I should know?"

"Jake's dad was the drunk driver who killed my husband," I told him next, almost chuckling at the astonishment that crossed his face. His expressions had otherwise been coolly detached. "Max obviously doesn't know that, either. My son has stopped talking due to trauma inflicted on him by my late husband, and Jake has sort of made it his mission to bond with him in an attempt to right that wrong."

"Okay, the blood pressure is starting to make more sense. I'm almost afraid to ask, but is there anything else?"

"Yeah…," I started, dragging the word out in a long exhale. "Jake declared his feelings for me last night, and I threw them back in his face pretty cruelly. I want you to understand that I don't believe I deserve someone as wonderful as him. He's been single-handedly taking care of his mom and her house, checking on the father, protecting his brothers from having to deal with any of that, worrying about my son and me, and holding down a full-time job. To say he's got a lot on his plate is just…yeah, I understand why his blood pressure is so high. And I feel responsible for pushing it to the breaking point."

With that, my calm exterior crumbled, and the tears I'd been holding back came out of me like floodwaters from a burst dam.

Chapter 34

LILY WAS A FORCE of nature. She dried my tears, found fresh tissues when I needed them, and kept replenishing my supply of water. She gave Max the same level of attentive care, pausing only to hug and reassure us. If I hadn't already blow-torched my chance of being part of this family, I would have been making plans to get to know her better. I desperately needed female friends, and she embodied every trait I could possibly want in a confidante and buddy. She even managed to draw me out, as I soon found myself confessing some of the awful things I'd said to Jake the night before.

"I don't deserve him," I finished, gripping a grossly damp tissue in my hand like a security blanket. "That's why I said those things. I screwed up when I married Dan, and I can't ever let myself trust another man again. Not even Jake. I'm too much of a mess. How could I ever trust my own judgment?"

"B-broken people d-don't deserve second ch-chances?" Max asked softly. "I'm l-lucky Lily didn't f-feel that way, because you'd have to s-search pretty hard to f-find someone more b-broken than me."

"No, Max, of course that's not what I mean," I said, immediately worried that he thought I was judging him. "It's different for me. I brought a child into an abusive situation, and it almost destroyed him. I owe it to Liam to never risk doing that again."

"*I* was the ch-child in the abusive s-situation that almost d-destroyed me," Max countered, the look in his eyes suddenly fierce. "J-Jake's the only r-reason I survived. The *only* r-reason. Pushing Jake away from you and L-Liam is doing w-way more harm than g-good, and you only h-have to look at m-me for p-proof. He's the b-best man in the w-world, M-Melody. I know you're s-scared, but if you l-let yourself l-love him, you'll n-never regret it. I s-swear it."

Before those words had a chance to soak into my rattled mind, a nurse appeared at the door.

"Jake Cruz's family?" she asked.

"Yes," Lily said as the three of us stood.

"We're waking him up now. The medicine finally got his blood pressure to decrease and stabilize. He's no longer in hypertensive crisis. He can have one visitor at a time. Maybe two, but you have to keep him from getting upset, okay? And only stay a few minutes."

Lily thanked her, and the nurse walked away as Max turned to me.

"Go ahead, M-Melody," he said. "He'll w-want to see you f-first."

"Oh, no—no way," I replied, shaking my head furiously. "You two go. You don't understand how badly I hurt him last night. I'm the last thing his stress levels need, trust me."

"I d-doubt that. But okay, we'll go. I'm g-going to ask him if he w-wants to see you, though. Okay? We'll let him d-decide."

I nodded, then returned to my chair after they left. Their hands were laced together in a tightly gripped display of unity. Seeing that made me remember how desperately I wanted what they had found in each other. Jake was right; the love between the two of them was a beautiful thing to witness.

Part of me believed what Max had told me—I knew in my heart that Jake was no Dan. He'd done nothing but show me, day after day, that kindness and patience were his default settings, not cruelty or judgment. But I'd surely destroyed any chances Jake and I ever had of being together. My cruelty had pushed him right off the edge of his emotional cliff. I didn't see how he could ever forgive me for that.

Several long minutes later—which I filled by pummeling myself with looping bouts of self-recrimination—Lily and Max came back, somewhat lighter looks on both their faces.

"How is he?" I asked, bracing myself for the frank admission that he didn't want to see me.

"He's Jake," Lily said with a soft laugh. "He was fussing about how long we've been here and apologizing for making us worry."

"That sounds about right," I said, smiling in spite of myself. *Of course* Jake was still worrying about Max. He was never *not* worrying about Max.

"And of c-course he s-said he wants to s-see you," Max told me. "Although he d-did look s-surprised when we t-told him you're h-here."

The smile that had just appeared was immediately wiped away again. "Yeah, I can understand his surprise, given how nasty I was to him last night."

"J-just be there f-for him, okay?" Max asked, his eyes pleading.

I nodded—yes, of course I understood. I couldn't again twist the knife I'd used last night to kill whatever had been growing between us. Not that I wanted to anymore. I needed time to consider what Max had told me and analyze the way I felt when I thought I might have lost Jake forever. There was a lot I still didn't know, and I still didn't really trust myself. But for some reason I trusted Max and Lily. They were both clearly convinced that Liam and I were safe in Jake's arms. I wanted to let myself feel that conviction, too.

I quietly crept into his room, a flashback suddenly pulling me to that night I'd met him at his father's bedside. His eyes were closed, but they popped open as I slowly approached. Then we studied each other for a long moment, a million unspoken emotions flickering tentatively between us.

"C'mere," he finally said, reaching out. I hesitated, nervous regrets skittering through my mind like attic mice. But I shook them away along with my doubts and self-recriminations as I climbed onto the bed next to him, laying my arm gently across his chest.

He wrapped his arms around me in return, and I squeezed my eyes shut in an attempt to fight back the tears that once again blurred my vision.

Chapter 35

Feeling Lucky

I'D BEEN LUCKY. *Extremely* lucky. Despite having sky-high blood pressure and a fairly impressive collection of gallstones, I didn't end up suffering a heart attack or a stroke. I also didn't wreck my car and possibly injure other people after passing out behind the wheel, didn't die like Dan, or end up in a coma like my old man.

No, I lived. With some blood-pressure medications, surgery to remove my gallbladder, and a renewed focus on lowering my stress, it looked like I'd be just fine—or so the doctors were telling me.

And my reward for all of that was currently snuggled into my arms on that hospital bed. There I was, somehow, being given the chance to lie in that bed and hold Melody in my arms, if only just that one time. Major medical scare in exchange for wrapping her tightly against me? Yeah, it was a good deal.

"I'm so sorry," she whispered. "This is all my fault, and you must hate me right now."

"Oh no you don't," I said. "I was stressed out and shoving my feelings down inside long before you came along. Seriously, Mel, I'm like a human pressure-cooker. I'm really, really good at it, actually. They recently invited me to join the pro circuit, although I don't want to brag about that too much."

I think that goofy joke pulled a laugh out of her, but since her face was still pressed into my side, it could have been a sob or a gasp. I mean, come on, I'm not nearly as funny as Max.

"Seriously, Jake, I got scared last night. I was overwhelmed, and instead of just talking with you about it, I lashed out. It wasn't fair of me to take my fears out on you like that, and none of what I said was true anyway."

"That's where you're wrong," I began, swatting away the hope that was starting to buzz around me. *None of what she'd said was true? Really?* Including about her lack of feelings for me? *No!* No way. I couldn't read into what she was saying. She simply felt bad that I might have died if I hadn't stopped the truck before I passed out. It was nothing more, and I had to shut those hopeful questions down hard. Given my current situation, I absolutely couldn't afford to let myself misinterpret what she was saying. Plus, I didn't think my heart could take another beating like that. "No, seriously, you *were* right. I've been controlling everyone's lives and taking away their freedom to make their own choices, at least where Mitch and Max are concerned. But wow, suddenly that's a huge joke, isn't it? Look at me right now. I'm doing a pretty crap job of dealing with my *own* life, so what made me think I could handle everyone else's, too?"

"No, Jake, no—you're absolutely *nothing* like Dan, and I'm serious that we need to talk about—" She stopped herself from finishing the rest of that thought when a nurse suddenly appeared in the room.

"Time's up," he said. "This guy needs a whole lot of peace and relaxation, although I have to say that the two of you look pretty happy and cozy in there. Come back again tomorrow and see him during visiting hours. I promise we'll take good care of him until you get back."

"Can I…that is, can I bring a child along?" Melody asked, gingerly pulling herself away from my side and out of the bed. I was dying to beg her to stay, but the nurse was right of course, and it was getting late. Melody needed to get back to Liam.

"No, not unrelated kids," the nurse said. "Not while he's in the critical care unit."

"He's my son," I said. I don't know what possessed me to do that, but even as the words marched confidently up and out of my throat, I knew I meant them. I glanced at Melody, daring her to contradict me, but I was met by a tender look instead. If women weren't such a persistent mystery, I would have sworn that I saw true love on her face. But after last night…well, I knew I wasn't seeing things quite right. I couldn't be.

"Your son?" the nurse said, now fiddling with the bags of medicine and fluids and whatever else was hanging off the machines at my bedside. "Sure, that's a different story, as long as he's over five. But of course, you two know him best. Some kids just can't handle hospitals. They're not ready for how scary and smelly they are, and they aren't able to keep quiet, either. As I said before, our patient here needs peace and relaxation."

"Oh, Liam will be quiet," I said, winking at Melody. "I guarantee it."

"Yeah," she said, a fully formed smile on her face now. "Very quiet."

The nurse nodded. "Okay, well, I'll let you say your goodbyes. Then I'll be back to check on you. Try to get some sleep."

As he walked out of the room, Melody approached my bed again and took my hand.

"Your son, huh?" she asked, gently playing with my fingers.

"Mel, you might not want to be a family with me, and I'm going to have to accept that and make peace with it. But don't keep Liam away from me. Please."

"There's a lot we need to talk about," she replied. "But no, I would never do that. He chose you the day he first climbed up on your lap. You're his as surely as he's yours."

I gave her hand a squeeze as she pulled back from me.

"See you tomorrow," she said.

I was dying to tell her again that I loved her, but I knew it was stupid to keep pushing the subject. We were friends, and I loved her son. That was going to have to be enough.

She backed up a few steps, gave me a last little wave, and turned to leave. When the door clicked shut, I couldn't help adding, "I love you" anyway.

The beep of my heart monitor was the only reply I received.

Chapter 36

Confessions and Confrontations

HE'S MY SON.

Jake's emphatic declaration electrified me. It might have even rewired my heart as well as my brain. I couldn't stop hearing those words or seeing the emphatic look on his face as he said them, as though he was fully prepared to battle for the right to be Liam's new father. His powerful and loving declaration stayed with me all that night and into the next day, rewinding and replaying and even weaving its way into my dreams. *He wants to claim Liam as his own....* Nothing before had ever felt so right.

Also, those words clicked firmly into my heart as surely as if they were a real, biological truth, because somewhere along the way, Liam had become Jake's son. There was no sense denying it or fighting it. It was in the patient way Jake read and re-read all of Liam's favorite books to him, and then read them again. It was in the endless games of catch or tag in the backyard, and in the help with homework that Jake generously gave. And, of course, the sweet snuggles in the recliner.

Jake had stepped into a fatherly role in Max's life, even as a teenager. So the man had a lot of practice being a parent; in some ways, he had even more experience than I did. He'd helped his brother weather countless emotional storms. And then, almost immediately after Max was standing on his own two feet, Jake started doing the same for Liam. Since the day they met, Jake had been busy picking up the broken pieces of my young son's heart and stitching them back together with his goofy jokes and persistent patience and devotion.

My sudden conviction that Jake belonged in Liam's life was a complete turnaround from what I'd told Jake the night before. And it was a complete turnaround from what I'd been telling myself all along, too. I knew how ridiculous it all was. Those arguments I'd used—the ones about never trusting another man with Liam—were what I'd used as justification for rejecting the love of this wonderful man. It turns out they had all the structural integrity of a house of cards. The truth of the matter was that I had been scared to trust my own heart to another man, and I'd used Liam as a convenient excuse. It had taken Jake's health scare to wake me up to the truth—I loved him. Of course I did. He was honest, dedicated, trustworthy, kind, and giving…and all of it at the expense of his own well-being.

Jake might not know it yet, but his days of putting everyone else's needs ahead of his own while he allowed himself to become the human pressure-cooker that he'd joked about were over. He needed someone in his life who would put him first and protect that generous heart of his. As for me, I had a lifetime of love buried inside and waiting to get out. It'd been stockpiling since the early days of my marriage, when Dan had slowly started repelling it and twisting it into something that eventually began to feel like hate instead. Jake needed to be loved and cared for, and I needed to be able to give my love to someone who would cherish it. We were perfect for each other.

But before I could go lay my soul on the floor in front of him, beg for him to forgive me and let me love him, there was someone I needed to talk to first. Two someones, actually, and I had a feeling they weren't immediately going to understand my desire to form a family with Jake: Celeste and Ron. They were Liam's only grandparents. And other than me—and now Jake—they were his only family. I'd never confided in them before, so there wasn't much chance they were going to be too thrilled with the idea that I found someone to love so soon after their son's death. But, at the very least, I owed them the truth.

*   *   *

I approached their door filled with self-recrimination wrapped in a thick layer of fear. Why hadn't I ever reached out to them before? I had to reveal some ugly truths about Dan; I didn't see any way around that. And the timing of those fact-bombs was surely going to seem highly suspicious to them. They'd likely think I was making up stories about their precious son to justify wanting to be with someone else.

By the time Ron pulled open the door and greeted me with a surprised but warm hello, I'd tangled myself hopelessly inside a knotted bundle of nerves.

"H-hi," I managed to splutter as he gestured for me to come in.

"Celeste!" he called. "Melody's here!"

"Melody!" she said as she swept elegantly into the room, her face mirroring the surprise I'd seen on Ron's. Judging by their reactions, I guess I'd never dropped by unannounced before.

"Is everything okay with the friend you needed to go see last night?" Celeste went on. "And with Liam? We had a wonderful night with him, by the way, and he looked happy enough this morning when we dropped him off at school."

"Oh yes, thank you," I replied, sitting gingerly on the edge of a fussy, overstuffed armchair after Celeste gestured toward it. "Thank you again for jumping in last minute like that. I appreciate it so much."

"Honestly, we'd love to do things like that more regularly, if that's something you'd be open to," she said. "Wouldn't we, Ron?"

"We would," he agreed, flashing a patient look at his wife as he joined her on the loveseat that was straight across from where I was tensely perched. "We love that boy."

"I know," I said, nodding. "And he loves the two of you. So, sure, I'd be happy to share more of his time with you. I never tried to keep you away but, well, it's always been hard for me to reach out to people. It's hard to accept help."

"We're here for you, Melody," Celeste assured me. "Please believe that's true. You can come to us with anything."

"Well...that's why I'm here today, actually," I said, grateful for the opening. "I need your help and understanding with something. But, well, like I just said, it's always been hard for me to reach out to you. I thought you'd...take Dan's side, I guess. I didn't think I could trust you, not really, no matter how bad things got."

"How bad what got?" Ron asked, surprising me by speaking up without first being prodded by Celeste.

I didn't know how to answer that question. I mean really, which bit of controlling domination that their son had doled out would convince them? Which instance of suffocating judgment?

In the end, I was too scared to hit them too hard with the truth of the matter. At least not without first presenting a little bit of evidence.

"Why do you think Liam stopped talking?" I asked.

Chapter 37

Ron and Celeste

"WHY DID LIAM stop talking?" Celeste echoed, her words a bit hesitant. "Because…well, because his father died, of course."

"No," I replied immediately. "Think back. He stopped talking before Dan died. Did Dan ever explain it to you? Did he ever give you a reason?"

"No," Celeste said, her face turning stubborn and stony. "You're confusing the timeline, Melody. That's not the way it happened."

"I'm not confusing anything here, because the day it happened is carved on my soul," I said, my fingers fidgeting nervously now. "Liam got a 79% on a math test that day, and Dan was furious about it. He made Liam sit at the table for hours, writing and rewriting every problem on the test, over and over. Then he made him do the same thing with all the problems in that chapter of the math textbook. Over and over and over. Liam was crying, and Dan told him that no son of his was going to get a 79 on a test. Liam just sat there, tears streaming down his face, rewriting those math problems. He's never said another word since that night."

Tears were coursing down Celeste's face now. "Why are you saying these things? You're twisting things and mixing them up in your mind. Yes, naturally, Dan could be firm, but boys have to have a firm upbringing!"

"He was more than firm. He was cold to us. Nothing we did was ever good enough for him. Nothing made him happy. Trust me, I never wanted to tell you these things. I never wanted to force you to see your son for who he really was. But you asked me recently how I could possibly be spending time with another man so soon after Dan's death, and the truth is, Dan killed the love inside me a long time ago. He killed my love, and he stole Liam's voice."

"No!" Celeste said, shaking her head furiously. "*No!* I know he wasn't perfect, but he was *my* baby, as surely as Liam is yours."

"I know that. Of course I know that. But your baby very methodically cut me off from all my friends. He forced me to quit my job and abandon my dreams of becoming a vet. He wouldn't allow my own mother to visit, and because of that she died alone, surely thinking I didn't love her anymore. All of that is the truth. I'm not twisting anything. I'm not changing any of the facts to suit my own narrative. I'm not. I'll admit, though, that I'm not highlighting my own failings, either. By not protecting my son well enough…well, I know I carry blame, too. I'm trying to forgive myself and move forward. I don't want to live in the past, and I don't want to rub your noses in the hard truth, either. So I won't say anything else negative about him, not to you and not to Liam. But I need you to understand where I'm coming from. I need you both to understand why, for the first time in my adult life, I feel free."

"Oh Melody," Celeste said, "this is about that man, isn't it?"

"Yes, in part it is. He's a wonderful person. He's used his experiences with his brother, who I think I mentioned to you, to help draw Liam out. He reads to him and plays catch with him and helps him with his homework. Jake's become a real, loving, supportive father figure to him."

"No!" Celeste said, and the fury in her tone caused me to jump. "I won't have it! You can't bring some stranger in and hand him Dan's life! That was all supposed to be his! You're Dan's *wife*, and Liam is Dan's *son!* That's Dan's home, too! Those are Dan's games of catch and Dan's books to read with Liam!"

"But that's what I'm trying to tell you—he never did those things, Celeste!" Tears welled in my eyes. I already regretted even attempting to make them understand, because of course they never really would. "Not once," I finished quietly.

"What are you saying then?" Celeste demanded. "You're going to pretend Dan never existed and run off with this guy?"

"I do love Jake," I said. "I won't lie to you about that. He's wonderful, and he loves us, too. But I'm not running anywhere. I'll honor Dan's memory by holding onto our relationship with the two of you. I meant it when I said that you're welcome to play a bigger role in Liam's life. He needs all the love and support he can get."

"I just don't see how you can sit there and speak that way about our son, the father of your child," she pressed on. "And now you somehow expect us to just go along with—"

"Enough!" Ron commanded, startling me again. "Celeste, *enough*. Enough pretending like we didn't know exactly what our son had become. We sat back and did nothing, even though we knew—don't deny it, because we both *knew*—how hard and cold and demanding he was. I don't know what happened to that boy. That's not the way he was raised. And I'm sorry, Melody. I'm sorry we never stepped in or called him on it. Of course you never came to us or trusted us before. In turning a blind eye, we were complicit."

I sat back in the chair, wide-eyed and absolutely stunned. That speech contained more words than I'd heard Ron speak cumulatively in the last decade.

"Of course I forgive you," I said. "I never blamed the two of you. Those mistakes were Dan's alone. But now, I just…I just want the chance to give Liam the father he deserves. I made some mistakes, and I tried to push Jake away, so I don't even know if he'll have me. But I love him. Liam loves him. I intend to beg his forgiveness and plead for a second chance. And if he somehow gives me that chance, I'm holding on and never letting go."

"I need time," Celeste said, even as Ron reached over and took her hand in his before looking back up at me.

"You've got our support on this," he told me. "Always."

Chapter 38

The Breakthrough

HOSPITALS SEEM to be designed to make sure you can't sleep. And just to increase the difficulty further, everyone applies a bunch of pressure about the topic, as though it's something you're merely refusing to do. They're all *Remember, the best thing you can do for yourself right now is sleep,* or *Rest is your ticket out of here.*

And yet those same people were in and out of my room all night long, checking on me, taking my vital signs, and playing with those bags of fluid hanging next to my bed. Then there was the racket my heart monitor was making. By the time Max appeared the next morning, I was starting to envy my dad's coma.

"You l-look like c-crap," he said, eyes narrowing as he approached.

"Oh darn, and here I am about to shoot the cover for *Hospitals Suck Weekly,*" I said. Remember, I was both sleep-deprived *and* not the funniest brother in the room.

"Seriously, though, you g-gonna be okay n-now?" he went on, worry creasing his face. "I c-can't do th-this without you, you kn-know."

"Do what?" I asked. "Be awesome?"

"D-do anything. Don't j-joke around about this, Jake. You s-scared me to d-death, and I d-don't want you to d-downplay the r-role you know you've p-played in my l-life. You're my b-brother, father, and b-best friend, all rolled up in one p-person. The *b-best* person."

"I love you, too, Maxwell," I said, my sleepy eyes getting watery now. "And I'll be right here for you as long as I possibly can. I'd do anything for you, including not driving my truck into a tree. Didn't you hear about the cool way I managed to stop it first before I fainted like a little girl who just spotted her celebrity crush? I'm practically as cool as you were with that whole 'attacking a knife-wielding thief' thing you did."

"Right," he said, a smile playing with the corner of his mouth now. "G-great job with th-that cool truck thing. B-but there's m-more going on here. Th-there's something you're n-not telling me. The d-doctors kept asking L-Lily and me about your s-stress levels. I c-couldn't think of a s-single thing to t-tell them, but when M-Melody showed up…well, f-from the l-look on her face, it s-seemed like the s-stress thing m-made a whole lot of sense to her. Wh-what does she know that w-we don't? What aren't you t-telling me?"

I nodded. "It's true. There's a ton of stuff I haven't told you about. A *ton.*"

"Why?" he asked, a look of hurt scurrying across his face before he managed to lock it down. "Why w-wouldn't you tell me e-everything?"

"Oh, lots of reasons," I said, the words coming out in a long exhale. "Part of me will always be in that fierce protective mode when it comes to you. I never want to burden you or worry you. That's a big part of it."

"And you c-can stop d-doing that. Yeah, we b-both know I l-leaned on you like a c-crutch for years. B-but you can s-stop n-now. You got m-me to the other s-side, remember?"

"I know, I know. And I'm not saying that I don't respect and admire the man you've become. It's just that…old habits die hard, I guess. And another part of my stress has to do with Melody, who I *have* talked with you about, by the way. You just don't know the latest news."

"Which is…?"

"I laid my heart out for her the night I landed in here. Told her I loved her and that I wanted to be a family with her and Liam."

"You l-look upset, b-but she told L-Lily and me a little b-bit about this in the waiting r-room," Max said. "But her v-version didn't sound s-so bad. Wh-what happened?"

"She told me what she said the last time I tried to talk feelings with her. She said we're only ever going to be friends. And I have to really hear her and believe her this time, because she said the reason she's shutting me down is because I'm too controlling, just like her husband was."

"*Y-you?*" Max asked, shock emanating off his face. "You're n-not controlling!"

"Yeah, I kind of am," I admitted. "I've been working so hard to protect you and Mitch from certain truths that I stole your freedom to make decisions for yourselves. She's right: I'm not worthy of her or her love. But, well, the shock of hearing her words is what did me in that night, I guess. My blood pressure shot right through the top of my head, and now here we are."

"N-no," he said, shaking his head. "She's wr-wrong. And wh-what do you mean about M-Mitch and me? What d-decisions? What f-freedom?"

"It's something I've been working overtime to protect you from," I started, my cadence halting as I tried to pull the right words out of the air. I didn't know how I should say all of it. In a quick, rip-the-bandage-off kind of way? Or slowly, with delicately chosen words aimed at softening the edges? I just didn't know.

"It's to do with Dad," I said finally.

Max's eyes widened even as a knock sounded at the door. The door opened, and Melody's beautiful face appeared around the side of it.

"Oh, Max, you beat us here!" she said. "Liam and I will be out in the waiting room. Let us know when you're done."

"N-no, come on in," he said with a wave. Then he shot me a classic *We're not done here* kind of look. After that, I turned my attention to the precious woman walking into the room, Liam trailing shyly behind her.

"He's a little nervous," she said. "I tried to tell him we could wait until they sent you home, but, well, it was clear he needed to see you for himself right away. I even pulled him from school, since it seemed so important to him.

"Well, don't just stand there, Luke!" I said, smiling broadly, with a wave to Max as he slipped out of the room. "Get on over here and give me a hug."

Liam looked over at me, nervousness flickering across his face, then up to his mom.

"It's just me, buddy," I said. "I know all these weird machines are scary, but I promise I'm the same guy as always."

His face turned red and blotchy as he fought the tears that were threatening to fall from his eyes. He looked back up at Melody again, and she gave him a reassuring smile. Then he broke free of his fears and scrambled across the room, up onto the bed, and right into my arms. None of that was the shocking part, though.

None of that was what caused both Melody and me to drop our mouths open in shocked wonder. No, it was because, as he latched his little arms around me and burrowed his face into my chest, he spoke his first word in months.

"Jake!"

That's when I knew everything was going to be okay.

Chapter 39

Hearing and Understanding

QUESTIONS SWIRLED in the air between us as my gaze locked with Melody's. I was filled with uncertainty: Should I acknowledge Liam's breakthrough? Was that the right way to handle it?

Melody simply nodded her head, as though she completely trusted me to handle that huge moment, which astonished me almost as much as Liam's voice had.

I tried not to wonder what that trust might signify as I nodded back at her, then I squeezed Liam again. He was still wrapped tightly around me like he never wanted to let go. I understood the sentiment, as that's pretty much how I felt about him *and* his mom. A pain twisted inside me at the reminder that, unfortunately, she didn't feel the same way. I could hear the rhythm on my monitor speed up, and I tried to push those regrets back out of my mind and force myself to calm down. Melody and Liam were there with me, after all, and that's all that mattered.

Liam finally picked his head up off my chest and peered up at me.

"I didn't know you could talk," I said, smiling down at him. "That was a pretty awesome surprise."

"You're sick," he said, his brow crinkling in worry. "My dad was in his car, and he went to Heaven. And my mom said you were in your car, and now *you're* sick."

I met Melody's stricken eyes, my panic surely radiating back at her. Although I never would have connected those dots on my own, his logic made sense. Of course he was drawing parallels here. I knew I needed to choose my next words very, very carefully.

"I'm sorry, kiddo," I said. "I would never scare you on purpose. But what happened with your dad and what happened with me are two different things. I know they probably *seem* similar, but in my case, I just need to take better care of myself, that's all. I'm okay, really. I'm not going to Heaven anytime soon. We'll be back at your house playing in the backyard before you know it."

He considered my explanation for a few moments, then said "Okay," the trusting innocence of youth helping him accept my words as a solid truth. "Today?"

"No, honey, not today," Melody jumped in with a laugh as she approached the bed and sat down next to us. "He still needs to rest. Jake, what are the doctors telling you about that?"

"They want to remove my gallbladder as soon as possible," I replied. "I've got gallstones that are blocking something…I don't know what, exactly. But it explains why my stomach has been in such bad shape lately that I can barely eat anything. I thought I had an ulcer, but gee, lucky me, it was this other problem instead. They said the gallbladder really needs to come out, but they had to get my blood pressure stabilized first. I'm a hot mess."

"Yeah," she said, reaching over to take my hand. "But you're *our* hot mess."

I looked at her, absolutely shocked. I know she thought of me as her best friend, but saying stuff like that wasn't exactly going to help mend my broken heart.

"You are," she insisted after seeing the doubt on my face. "I've got some news about that, too, but it's not necessarily appropriate for little ears. Let's just say that I made some realizations recently. And I faced a few demons while I was at it."

"Oh, yeah, sure, that cleared things right up," I teased, utterly confused.

"Sorry, I just don't want to, umm...." She nodded her head knowingly toward Liam. "But I had a very long and very overdue talk with Ron and Celeste after your declaration. And after what you said about Liam."

"Huh? What I said about Liam?" I asked, even as my words from the previous day came flooding back to me. "Wait, you mean about when I…uh, claimed him as my own?"

"Yeah," she said, giving my hand a squeeze. "I let them know that things are changing. That things *have* changed, and they're going to have to accept that."

Joy leapt wildly inside me for a brief moment—was she saying that she told Dan's parents I was in her life now?!

But then her other words came back to me, right along with a cold slap of reality: *We're only ever going to be friends.* She'd said that over and over. When was I going to start actually *hearing* her? Clearly, she was just talking about telling Dan's parents that I'd be playing a fatherly role in Liam's life. Obviously, that's all she meant.

"Oh, yeah, good," I said, squeezing her hand in return before drawing my fingers back out of her grasp. "I definitely meant what I said. I'm here to stay in his life."

"No, it's more than that," she shot back. "It's—"

Then the door opened again, and Dr. Aquino breezed into the room.

*　　*　　*

"Who do we have here?" he asked.

"Liam and Melody," I said, avoiding explanations of just who they were to me, especially since I wasn't exactly sure myself. "How's everything looking?"

"Good, good." He stared at the tablet in his hands. "Your vitals have stabilized, and your blood pressure is good. So now it's time to get that gallbladder out. The nurses will be starting your surgery prep. You haven't had anything to eat, right?"

"No," I said, watching as Melody stood up and tugged at Liam's arm to get him to do the same.

"We'll be back soon," she said. "C'mon, Liam, let's let Jake talk to his doctor. Jake, we're going to finish this talk after your surgery."

"Don't worry," the doctor chirped, still focused intently on the screen in front of him. "He's in good hands."

Liam begrudgingly climbed down, and I watched as they both walked to the door. I gave them a little smile and wave as they disappeared out of sight.

As hard as it was to watch them leave, I was honestly kind of grateful for the doctor's interruption. I was too weary to face another one of Melody's reminders that we'd never be able to cross the river of friendship that separated us.

She'd said all that before, and I just needed to learn to live with the truth.

# Chapter 40

Waiting Room Confidences

LIAM IS TALKING AGAIN!

Despite my worry about Jake and this latest surgery hurdle on his road to recovery, I was floating on a dreamy rush of relief and joy as Liam and I made our way to the waiting room.

Max wasn't there, but I stopped anyway, crumpling onto one of the thinly upholstered chairs like a marionette before pulling Liam into my arms.

"Oh baby," I said, even as a part of me wondered if it was better not to call attention to the fact that he'd taken this huge step. "I was so happy to hear you talking to Jake."

If he had a reply to that, I might possibly have been squeezing him so hard that he couldn't find the air to say it. So he wrapped his arms around me and squeezed right back instead.

"I was so scared," he said finally, squiggling out of my embrace. "I don't want Jake to go to Heaven. He's nice to me. He plays with me, and he never yells."

"Yep, he's pretty awesome, but he's not headed to Heaven anytime soon. Jake's doctor said he's doing better. You were right there, so you heard him say that, too. Jake's doing so much better now that the doctors can fix something that was making his tummy hurt when he tried to eat."

"Okay," he said. "Can he come read to me tonight?"

"Soon, honey," I said, chuckling at his impatience. "Not tonight, but soon."

Max walked into the room then, a water bottle in his hand.

"H-hey, what's g-going on?" he asked, a trace of alarm hanging from his words. "Jake's still okay, right?"

"Yeah. Actually, his blood pressure is stable enough now that they're prepping him for the gallbladder surgery. Our visit got cut short when the doctor showed up."

"Oh, okay, g-good. Uh, M-Melody, c-can I talk to you?" He nodded toward Liam. "M-maybe across the r-room?"

"Okay, sure, but ignore this bit of impressively awesome parenting you're about to witness," I said. Then I pulled my phone out of my purse and opened a word-game app that Liam likes to play when he's given screen time. "Liam, here, play this for a few minutes. Max and I will be over there so we don't bother you."

I kept his screen time so limited that this represented a huge and unexpected treat, so I wasn't surprised when he jubilantly snatched the phone out of my hand on his way to zombie-like levels of entrancement.

"Trust me, he's good to wait now," I said as Max tried—but failed—to hide a snicker. "You laugh now, but just you wait until you have kids of your own. And speaking of kids, guess what? Liam started talking again!"

"Wh-what?!" Max said, his eyes comically large now. "When?"

"Just before, when we were visiting with your brother," I said. "Liam ran across the room, jumped in Jake's arms, and spoke for the first time in months."

"Wow, I'm s-so happy for you g-guys."

"Thanks." I was swiping a bit of the happiness that had started leaking from the corners of my eyes as we crossed the room and sat in chairs facing each other, mine angled so I could keep an eye on Liam.

"So what's up?" I asked.

"What w-was his first w-word?" Max asked.

"It was your brother's name," I said. "Of course."

"That s-sounds about right," he said, another chuckle falling from his mouth. "Actually, it f-fits with what I w-wanted to talk with you about. J-Jake has been like a f-father to me all my life, so this is c-coming from a place of l-love and concern for him. I'm s-scared that he won't b-be able to d-decrease his stress enough to s-stay healthy. And I d-don't even know wh-what's got him s-so stressed out, although I'm g-guessing you do. He said it has s-something to do with our d-dad, but I also kn-know that he t-told you he l-loves you, and you k-kicked him to the curb."

I tried to interject there, to tell him that I wasn't going to lie to myself or Jake any longer. To tell him that his brother's heart would get nothing but tender care in my hands from now on. Well, if he ever again took a chance and offered it to me again, that is. But as Max saw I was about to talk, he gestured for me to stop.

"P-please, j-just let me say this," he went on. "T-talking isn't my s-strong suit, as maybe you've f-figured out, and I was on a roll there."

"Yes, you were," I said with a short laugh. "Okay, yeah, let me have it. But there's more you don't know."

"Yeah, turns out th-there's a *t-ton* of stuff I d-don't know. The truth is, I'm f-frustrated with him. I th-thought he knew he c-could talk to m-me. But c-clearly he doesn't either know or b-believe it. He j-just bottles everything up until h-he explodes, apparently."

"I agree we need to try to help him work on that," I replied. "It came close to being his fatal flaw. Much, much too close."

"I d-don't know wh-what I would d-do without him, I really d-don't," Max said with a wince of pain. "And I c-can't imagine why you d-don't love a w-wonderful person like him back. B-but please, just don't j-jerk him around, okay? Obviously, n-none of this was your f-fault, but whatever you s-said that n-night, it w-was too much. Too h-harsh or too...s-something. I d-don't know. I'm s-simply asking you to p-please be kind to h-him. You don't have to l-love him back, of course, but d-don't destroy him, either."

"Oh Max, I've made a *lot* of mistakes in my life," I began, unable to stop the flow of words now, regardless of whether he was done. "A lot of mistakes. I married an abusive man, brought a child into that unstable home, let my abuser cut me off from the entire world including my own mother, and allowed my dreams to be put aside. But every bit as much as I regret all of that, I truly regret the things I said to Jake that night. You're right that he didn't deserve them. And you're right that he's the best man in the world. I've known him for such a short amount of time, but, like you, I can't imagine living without him now. Honestly, I was just scared to love or trust again, and I lashed out that night because of those fears. But I do love him, I really do. I knew it anyway, but almost losing him made that truth blindingly, unavoidably clear to me. And once he's out of surgery, I plan to beg his forgiveness and plead for a second chance."

"This t-turnaround isn't just g-guilt, is it? Or ggratitude, since L-Liam started talking again, and his f-first word was my brother's name?"

"I feel both of those emotions, sure," I admitted. "The fact that my son loves and trusts Jake so much that he gave him his first words following so much trauma? Yes, of course that means the world to me. But even if Liam wasn't a part of this equation, I'd love Jake anyway. He's patient, kind, and loving. He believes in me and supports my dreams. I could never find a better man if I hunted for the rest of eternity."

"Yeah," Max said, a look of relief shining in his eyes now. "H-he really needs to h-hear you say those th-things. As m-much as I want to p-pry this secret out of him, I th-think you should go t-talk to him f-first when he c-can have visitors again."

"Unfortunately, I have to go," I said. "Even though he'd love it, I can't just sit here all afternoon while Liam drains the battery on my phone. But of *course* I want to talk to Jake as soon as possible. I'm going to see if his grandparents can keep him overnight again. They're going to be so happy to hear him speaking, and I need to share that news with them, regardless. You take your turn and please let him know I'll be here as soon as I can. I promise you, if Jake's willing to forgive me for the awful things I said and trust me enough to give me a second chance, I'm going to hold onto him and never let go."

"Good," Max said, settling back in his chair with a look of satisfaction on his face.

Max had believed my words, but then he didn't know exactly how cruel I'd been that night. As I said goodbye and gathered Liam and my phone up, a persistent worry kept clattering through my head.

Max believes me...but will Jake?

Chapter 41

Telling Max

MAX'S FACE WAS the first thing I saw when I opened my eyes.

I had a moment of fuzzy forgetfulness before all the truths and memories came flooding back—Melody's words and their harsh slap of reality, my soaring blood pressure, my first time hearing Liam's precious voice, and then the gallbladder surgery.

Max's thumbs were flying across his phone, and he had a dopey, lovesick look on his face.

"Lily's at work?" I asked, wincing with discomfort as I also tried to stretch and reposition myself.

"J-Jake!" he said, putting the phone down and turning a relieved smile my way. "You're awake! Hey, t-take it easy. Th-that looked like it hurt."

"Nah, I'm good," I assured him, after which his face turned stormy.

"You're d-doing it again! You're awake f-five seconds, and you're already t-trying to p-protect me f-from the truth!"

"Okay, okay, yeah, that hurt a little," I said. "A *little*. But sorry, man. Bad habit."

"W-well knock it off," he said. "I m-mean it. You b-bottling everything up is wh-what landed you here in the f-first place, remember? That, and n-not taking c-care of yourself. You honestly th-thought it was n-normal that you c-couldn't eat anything w-without severe s-stomach pain? H-how did I m-manage to s-stay alive all th-those years when my primary g-guardian was using th-that kind of top-notch p-problem-solving and attention to d-detail?!"

"Dumb luck?" I offered, trying for a joke even though Max had quietly, yet fiercely, hurled those words at me in anger, something he had never done before. Angry Max was a stranger to me, but it was kind of nice to meet him. Even though I had known for years that he certainly must have a steel backbone to have survived that childhood, it was still gratifying to see his grit and fire on display.

"Don't," he said. "Don't j-joke around or t-try to distract me. You n-need to release that p-pressure inside of you. And you n-need to stop b-bottling it up to begin with. S-start by finishing our c-conversation from b-before. What have you b-been hiding from Mitch and me? This is wh-what you were upset about the n-night we w-went to d-dinner with L-Lily and Claire, isn't it?"

"Yeah, it was on my mind then. And yes, you were right when you asked if I was holding something back from you that night."

"It's time," he said. "It's time to s-stop carrying whatever this b-burden is alone. What d-don't we know about Dad? Did he h-hurt you? Is th-that it?"

"No, relax, that's not it. But yeah, he hurt someone. Almost—it's been now, maybe five or six months ago?—the old man got loaded one night and got behind the wheel of his car. He was drunk, and he slammed into an oncoming car. He killed a man. A man with a wife and young son."

All the color drained from Max's face. "Oh no. Th-that's...that's just h-horrible. And so not what I g-guessed you m-might say. I take it D-dad walked away unscathed?"

"No," I said, then closed my eyes to the pain I could see on Max's face. I also had to collect my thoughts for a moment before pushing on. "He's in a coma, Max. Right here in this hospital, as a matter of fact. He might have brain damage. Even if he wakes up, he might never be the same."

"Gee, that'd be a sh-shame," Max said, and we both found ourselves chuckling—couldn't really help it—at his dark humor. He wasn't wrong, after all; this wasn't exactly a huge loss to society. Nevertheless, Max went on with, "No, f-forget I s-said that. He's a h-human being, and I don't want to s-stoop to his l-level. Anyway, I can't b-believe you hid all of that. I c-can't even g-guess why you did it or what you th-thought you w-were accomplishing."

"Just didn't want to set you back, Maxwell," I told him with total honesty. Nevertheless, my reason suddenly sounded flimsy and thin, even though it held back an avalanche of truth for so long. "There you were, falling in love with the girl of your dreams, embracing speech therapy, and coming out of your shell. I didn't want absolutely anything—like, I don't know, bad memories or misplaced guilt or sorrow—knocking you off the course you'd set. So I just dealt with it all myself."

"W-wait, that's why you've b-been mowing their g-grass," he said, the puzzle pieces coming together in his mind.

I shrugged. "Yeah, although I'm really bad at it. I also handle their bills. And I check in on them both daily."

"S-so absolutely n-no one else kn-knows? You've c-carried all of those b-burdens alone?"

"Well, no," I said. "I mean, you know, Mom knows."

At that, we both shared another chuckle. Mom knowing was the same as no one knowing, something Max was painfully aware of, unfortunately.

"There's more though," I continued. "One more big secret, and in some ways it's the biggest and most impactful of all."

"Are you s-serious? What m-more could there p-possibly be?"

"That man Dad killed?" I started, only continuing after Max nodded his head. "He was Melody's husband."

Max full-on gasped, at which point I couldn't help chuckling again.

"J-Jake, don't laugh," he said. "S-sorry about the over-the-top r-reaction, but come on! Wh-what are the ch-chances? Or w-wait, did you m-meet her before or after he d-died?"

"After," I said. "Of course. She showed up here at the hospital to whisper her thanks to him. Thanks for freeing her and Liam from their abuser. And then...well, I guess we were drawn to each other instantly."

"N-no wonder," he said, shaking his head. "I totally g-get it n-now. It's no w-wonder you almost exploded t-trying to k-keep all this in."

Once again, despite the seriousness of the situation, I found myself letting out a small laugh as relief flooded through me. Telling Max all my secrets felt better than I could have imagined, and it lifted a huge weight off my shoulders.

Of course, now I just had to tell Mitch. And then I had to learn to live without Melody.

At that thought, I suddenly wasn't feeling so light and carefree anymore.

Chapter 42

Hallway Therapy

"OH H-HEY," Max said as we practically collided outside Jake's room. I'd dropped off Liam with Ron and Celeste—who had been every bit as delighted by Liam's breakthrough as I expected—before dashing back to the hospital to have my long-overdue talk with Jake. They were astonished when Liam started jabbering away at them as though the silence had never happened. When I told them about Jake's role in his sudden turnaround...well, I was starting to have the feeling that they'd come around to welcoming Jake into the family more easily than I had feared.

"I w-was just h-headed home," Max went on. "L-Lily and I are g-going to grab some d-dinner."

"Okay, good timing then. My turn to talk to him, right?"

"Yeah, h-he's all yours."

"I *hope* he'll be all mine," I said. "I really, really want us to be a family. I'm praying he'll forgive me. Actually, I was practicing my speech all the way over here."

Max smiled. "He w-will. You won't need a p-perfect speech; he's a pretty f-forgiving guy. He and I h-had a long talk after you l-left. Actually, after l-lecturing you about the importance of b-being k-kind to him, I ended up sort of r-ripping into him about how he n-needs to stop k-keeping secrets and b-bottling up his emotions."

"Good! I plan to stage a similar intervention with him. Well, you know, plus I'll do all that groveling stuff I told you about."

"That's p-perfect. Maybe if we all t-team up and k-keep saying the s-same things to him, he'll start to b-believe and understand how s-serious this is. And then m-maybe he'll stop h-holding back all his emotions and secrets from us."

I nodded. "Liam and I want him to stick around for a really, really long time. Liam's gotten so attached to him. Actually, did Jake mention that Liam drew some mental parallels between his father's death and Jake's fainting episode in his truck? Liam's terrified he's going to die like his dad did."

"Oh no, th-that's so sad," Max said, remorse and regret mingling on his face now. "No, he d-didn't tell me that. I'm s-sorry that Liam's scared, and I'm s-sorry for everything you've b-been through. J-Jake *did* finally tell me about h-how your h-husband died. I kn-know that my d-dad is responsible. I'm s-so sorry that our f-family brought so much p-pain and heartache to yours."

"Thank you for saying that Max," I said with a sigh. Our families were wrapped up in such a tangle of Shakespearean devastation that it was hard to grasp or vocalize the enormity of it all. "It's such a complex tragedy, though, and my feelings about it are probably going to take years of therapy to unravel."

"For all of us," Max replied, a rueful smile lifting the edge of his mouth as he nodded.

"Right. There are so many ways to look at it, and I'm sure you're already feeling a lot of this. On the one hand, it's kind of easy to simply be happy that two really awful men took each other out of our lives, you know? But on the other hand, if we truly believe in things like second chances—like the one I'm praying Jake gives me—then it's all just awful. Dan never gets a do-over, you know what I mean? He was robbed of any opportunity to realize his mistakes and become a better father and husband. It's just over for him; that's it, time's up. Of course, he never showed any signs at all that he was ever *going* to change, but who knows what age and wisdom might have given him? And we don't have a crystal ball when it comes to the situation with your dad, but it's kind of looking like there aren't going to be any opportunities for second chances for him either. So, yeah, a huge part of me is honestly grateful for my freedom. And for Liam's freedom. But I'd be lying if I said that there wasn't a small part of me that's...just sad, I guess."

"I g-get it," Max said. "T-trust me, I do. My f-feelings about my f-father are complicated in p-pretty much the same ways. I don't th-think J-Jake knows this, but I can r-remember a time when my dad p-played with me and l-loved me. B-before I started s-stuttering. I m-miss *that* guy. B-but he died a l-long time ago. Part of me is g-glad the man he became m-might die, but the rest of me f-feels like a m-monster for saying that."

"You're not a monster any more than I am," I told him. "I think it's okay if we're both a little conflicted about this accident and the fallout from it. But I don't think it's bad that neither one of us will ever really miss them. I really don't."

"I agree," he said. "Th-thank you for what you j-just said. I'm glad we had this ch-chance to talk. And hey, I actually have a l-little *good* news."

"Oh, please tell me! I need all the good news I can get."

"They're talking about sending J-Jake home

tomorrow," he said. "L-looks like his l-little vacation is just about over."

"Vacation, oh no!" I said, struck by a fear I hadn't considered before.

"Said n-no one, ever," Max replied, humor sparkling in his eyes.

A small laugh bubbled out of me at his unexpected joke. "Sorry, but that word just reminded me of something: Did anyone contact the gym the day Jake was admitted? Is his job okay, or did he get in trouble for being a no-show?"

"No worries, I c-called them r-right away. And then I told J-Jake it was j-just more proof that he can s-start relying on m-me and confiding in me. I'm not that h-helpless kid who w-was afraid to m-make a phone call anymore."

"No, you're definitely not. Actually, talking to you has helped me so much. Can I get a hug? I need some confidence before facing Jake."

"Of course," he said, leaning in and wrapping his arms around me. "You've g-got this. You two are g-going to be as happy as L-Lily and I are. You'll s-see."

As I hugged him back, I silently prayed that he was right.

Chapter 43

Two Issues

I KNEW I WAS LYING there in that hospital bed because I was someone who desperately needed to chill out and repel stress. Unfortunately, change isn't so easy, and it wasn't long before I was right back to my usual clenched fist of emotions. Max had left for dinner with Lily, leaving me alone to stew in my own juices, which of course was always a dangerous place to be.

Part of me was upset because I didn't know how to mourn the death of my imaginary future with Melody and Liam. It's one thing to mend a broken heart when you can crawl off into a solitary hole, curl into the fetal position, and lose yourself in alcohol and sad songs. But I had no intention of cutting the two of them out of my life completely—especially Liam—so there could be no solitary grieving period either way. That boy needed me as much as Max ever had, and there's no way I would let him down, broken heart notwithstanding.

So I guess that meant I'd feel like a raw, open wound for a long time. After all, I couldn't even imagine a world where I'd be with Melody and not feel this way about her. Some part of me would always love her; that much I knew. The old me would have simply shoved those feelings down so they could bubble and boil with all their other little stress buddies. But this was supposed to be the new and improved me. *This* me couldn't shove those emotions down. No, I had to grow and evolve and somehow find other ways to heal my broken heart while still interacting with Melody.

The other problem was that I couldn't figure out how to tell Mitch everything that'd been going on lately. He deserved more than a text. More than a phone call, even. Maybe a phone call with video? That would probably work, except Max should be there, too. After all, the man lying in a coma on the sixth floor of the hospital, and the source of most of our problems, was also *their* dad. I had to stop owning everything and learn to depend on both of my brothers. So, yeah, ideally, they both should be there.

The two issues currently on my mind—those to do with Melody and those to do with Mitch—were making my old familiar pains twist and ache inside again, and I could hear my heart monitor starting to beep out warnings, which in itself was stressing me out. When was I going to learn how to control my emotions in a healthy way? The doctor mentioned they were planning to send me home the next day; I had to learn some new survival skills quickly if I didn't want to end up right back in the emergency room. I closed my eyes tight, listening to the beeps of the monitor, as I tried to force myself to calm down.

I was focusing so hard on it, in fact, that I didn't hear anyone come in until the door clicked shut. Then my eyes flew open to find Melody standing there, alarm flickering across her face.

"Jake? What's wrong?"

"Oh, hey Mel," I said, trying to sound casual, even though the mere sight of her made the pain in my chest squeeze hard again. "How's Liam?"

"He's fine," she said, crossing the room to sit next to me. "But don't change the subject. What's wrong?"

"I'm not going to be able to master stress control

after a day or two just because everyone says I need to," I confessed with a shrugged attempt at nonchalance. "So I'm doing what I always do—worrying."

"Oh Jake," she said, reaching for my hand now. I considered yanking it back; she really needed to stop sending me mixed signals if Project Eradicate Heartbreak was ever going to get off the ground. But in the end, I decided to allow myself the luxury of touching her again, if only for one last time. "What are you worrying about?"

I sighed. "A couple things. Mitch is part of it. I don't know how to tell him about all this stuff. Like I literally don't know how to tell him: Text? Phone call? Carrier pigeon? It's complicated because I kind of want Max there. Well, honestly, it'd be nice to have you and Lily both there as well. But how? As we all know, Mitch isn't exactly Mr. Communication, so passing a phone around isn't ideal."

"Jake, seriously? Come on, that's easy. Let's do a video call. You know, like the ones remote workers do every single day?"

"Oh, yeah...right." Her idea was so obvious and brilliant that it made me feel ridiculous for having labored over it. "That way he can meet you—your family is as much a part of this whole drama as ours, after all—and we can all update him together."

"There you go. I'm sure Max and Lily will be happy to join. That one was easy to handle. See how much it helps to open up to other people and bounce things off them once in a while?"

"Yeah," I said, still feeling foolish. "Thanks. That was a perfect solution."

"Okay, so that was one issue—but you said other things were on your mind, too. So come on, keep going. Don't think I didn't notice your heart monitor was freaking out when I walked in here, and don't even bother denying it. Just get it all out, Jake. That's got to be your new default setting, so start practicing."

"I'll work on it. I promise. But you aren't the right person to offer me advice on what else is bothering me. I need to talk to Max about it, I think."

"By any chance, is this about us?" she asked, a gentle look in her eyes that I didn't understand given her feelings for me. Or I should say *lack* of feelings for me.

"What are you talking about? There *is* no us."

"Jake, whatever you're thinking or feeling or worrying about, just stop, okay?" she said, tightening her hold on my hand. "That's what I came here to talk to you about. I'm so sorry I said those things the other night. I didn't mean to hurt you the way I did. I was just scared, and instead of facing those fears, I freaked out like an animal caught in a trap."

"Except you were right. I was being too controlling. I totally understand why you want nothing to do with me beyond friendship."

"You are *nothing* like Dan," she fired back immediately, her eyes sparking with emotion. "*Nothing!* I meant it when I told you that I was simply scared that night. I lashed out at you, but I'm so sorry for the things I said. I don't believe any of that nonsense, and neither does anyone else."

"Don't, Mel," I said, pulling my hand from hers now. "I know I gave everyone a scare, but I don't need you saying stuff to me out of regret or fear or whatever. I know where we stand, okay? I get it. No backtracking necessary. I'll figure out how to get over it eventually, but you've got to stop sending mixed signals. Please? I won't abandon Liam, but you've got to give me some space and let me heal before I can be ready for things to go back to normal between us."

"No!" she said, shaking her head now. "You're not hearing me. I don't *want* things to go back to how they were. I'm not simply feeling guilty or worried or whatever. I'm not. This isn't guilt talking. It's not gratitude that you're alive or that Liam broke his silence. I mean, yeah, of course I feel those things, too. But Jake, I was *scared* that night. Love and trust aren't exactly easy for me, and you know precisely why. Somehow, though, you broke through my fears, and you found a way to help me start to heal."

"So what are you saying?" I asked, afraid to unshackle the hope that was currently locked deep inside me. "You're going to have to spell it out for me."

"I was wrong to push you away," she said firmly. "Okay? *Wrong.* I mean, yeah, we're friends. But I think we're soulmates, too. That's right, I said *soulmates.* There are no mixed signals here, I swear it. I'm saying it as clearly as I possibly can—I don't want to be merely friends with you. I want *forever* with you. I want us to be a family. I love you, honey. I *adore* you, and I want to spend the rest of my life showing you exactly how true those words are and how sorry I am that I hurt you."

"You...you're serious?" I asked as hope started to break free and flutter around in my chest. "Because, Melody, you have to know I meant everything I said to you that night. I will cherish you and support you and never, ever try to take any of your freedoms away from you. That means my love won't ever be conditional. You can work or go to school or do anything you want, as long as you come home to me—and as long as you let me love you."

"I want that too," she said, wiping away the tears that had slipped down her cheeks and over those freckles I love so much. "And I'll do all those things for you, too. I'll support you and be there for you and your brothers. I'll love you, and I'll help you find ways to manage all that stress you've been carrying around. But you won't have any reason to build up those emotions again anyway, because your days of taking care of everyone except yourself are over. I'm going to be right there at your side, taking care of you and loving you."

I smiled and reached for her hand again. "If I wasn't so sore, I'd jump right out of this bed and take you in my arms right now. I'd kiss you right into our forever."

"Don't move," she said, crawling onto the bed next to me. "Because I like where your head's at right now."

I chuckled and wrapped my arms around her as happiness flooded through me. When she met my lips with a kiss so fiery that it made it sound like my heart monitor was about to explode, a sense of rightness shoved all the old, familiar pains right out of my chest.

With Melody in my arms as well as my heart, managing those emotions suddenly didn't seem like an impossible task anymore.

Chapter 44

The Video Call

MY NERVES were thrumming the day of our video call with Mitch. I was nervous to lay everything on the line for him, and I was scared that he'd let me down. I was terrified he wouldn't care.

I'd been slowly building resentment against him over the years, something I could only see and acknowledge now because of my new awareness of precisely how much of a mess I was. And about how unhealthy it was for me to pack that kind of negativity deep inside. My stint in the hospital had gifted me with clear insight; it was like I could now strap on my stress-o-meter goggles and see the world as it really was. Or at least *my* place in it, and the way I'd tried to take on everyone else's burdens and pains. Somehow, instead of lessening the pain levels, I'd managed to increase them.

But the simple fact that I resented the way Mitch had so effectively done a "peace out" disappearing act from our lives made me feel bad, too. I mean, come on. He's my twin. It's almost impossible to explain this to someone who isn't a twin, but...well, it kind of felt like I resented *myself*.

One by one, my family members joined the call. Melody and Max rang in at the same time, then Lily joined, too, with Claire visible in the background, which I wasn't expecting.

"Claire?" I asked, not bothering to hide my confusion. *"You're* stuck in the middle of this now?"

"Lily and I were hanging out and having a little girlfriend time," she said with a shrug. "I was going to leave, but I kind of wanted a peek at the Jake-a-like first. But then Lily asked me to stay. If you guys want me gone, though, I'm gone."

"I'm sorry, Jake," Lily said. "I was hoping no one would mind. She's my family, so I didn't think twice about asking her."

"If you need her support, Lils," I said, "then she stays."

"Thanks," Lily said even as the last member of our family rang in—Mitch was connecting to the call.

When his face appeared on the screen, I was surprised that a feeling of relief surged through me. Resentful of him or not, it sure was good to see his face.

"Whoa!" Claire whispered, although she must have been right by the microphone because it came through loud and clear. "Lily, girl you weren't kidding. The two of them together on my screen...I can't. It's too much pretty. I can't even look directly into it, like together they form the sun or something."

"Right?" Lily asked even as Max cut into their squealing.

"I'm right here, L-Lily," he said. "I can h-hear you ogling my b-brothers."

"Oh, you know you're the truly handsome one, my love," Lily said.

"Hey, Lily," Mitch said with a chuckle. "So the rumors were true, huh? You found your man?"

"Hi Mitch!" she said, her usual bounciness on full display. "Thank you again so much for everything you did to help Max and me find our way to each other. We are extremely happy and so deeply in love, and we owe so much of that to you."

"Hey!" I said, hoping to interject some humor. "What about me? *I'm* the one who got that ball rolling."

"Sure you did, honey," Melody said teasingly. "Everyone knows you probably helped, too."

"Yeah, s-seriously, Mitch," Max cut in, ignoring me completely. "Thank you s-so much. I've n-never been happier."

"You have no idea how happy that makes me, little brother," Mitch said. "Is that what this call is about? An update on how well our baby brother is doing?"

"Uh, no...." I started, and at that exact moment Liam's head popped into the screen on Melody's camera. He then let out a sound that landed somewhere between a shout and a wind-tunnel gasp.

"Mom!" he yelled way too loudly for the microphone. "Look! There's two Jakes!"

"That's right, little man, it's me, Jake," Mitch said, a smirk on his face.

"Mitch, c'mon man, don't mess with him," I said. "Liam, buddy, this is my twin brother, Mitch."

"Hi," Liam said softly, looking shy now. He disappeared with a little wave when Melody shooed him out of the room followed by an apology for the interruption.

"So, are any of you going to tell me what's going on?" Mitch asked. "I don't even know half the people I'm looking at right now. Is everything okay? Wait...is this an intervention or something? Did I become a raging alcoholic without knowing it?"

"Yeah, it *is* an intervention, but not for you," Melody said. "Hi, Mitch, I'm Melody. That was Liam, my son. I'm Jake's, uh—"

"Girlfriend and the love of my life," I finished after she stalled, chuckling at the shock on Mitch's face.

"Get out of here," he said. "I knew Maximillian went and fell in love, but not you, too. What are they putting in the water over there?"

"I don't know, but much like Max, this is the happiest I've ever been," I said.

"That's great," he replied, his tone tinged with just a hint of wistfulness. "I'm so happy for you guys. But if it's not simply a Max update and girlfriend announcement, then seriously: What's going on?"

"It's m-more like what *isn't* g-going on," Max said, beating me to it. "First of all, J-Jake has been c-carrying around a huge s-secret about Dad."

"*Dad?*" Mitch repeated, the color draining out of his face. "Wait, so Jake knows about Dad?"

"Yeah," I said. "Wait, what? *You* know about Dad too?"

"Yeah, man, I've known for years," he said. "I can't believe you told Max, though. That's what I was trying to prevent."

"Years?" I said. "Wait...what are you talking about? This only happened like five or six months ago."

"I thought...." Mitch started, then trailed off. "Wait, what are *you* talking about?"

"Ahh, family communication," Claire whispered to Lily, causing Max to chuckle.

"Who are you, again?" Mitch asked. "Because I thought I was talking to my family."

"Oh, you are," Claire said. "I'm Lily's friend, Claire."

"Right," he said, his tone suddenly sarcastic. "Congratulations."

"Thanks, I worked so hard to get to this moment," she said, her voice filled with a cutting edge I'd never heard in it before in response to Mitch's rudeness.

"Really feels like it's all paying off at last."

"I'm so happy for you," he said.

"Can we focus here?" I demanded, still astonished because, unless I misunderstood him, Mitch had been carrying around his own, separate secret relating to Dad for a while now. "Yes, Lily has a friend over, and no one minds except you, Mitch, so try to deal with it. And while you're struggling with that, tell me—what secret did *you* think we were talking about?"

"Nothing," he said quickly. A little *too* quickly. "I misspoke. Tell me what's going on, because you're starting to freak me out."

"Dad's in a coma," I told him, cutting straight to the point. "He has been since the night he got drunk and swerved into oncoming traffic."

"What?!" Mitch cried, his shock leaving no room for doubt that this was *not* the secret he was talking about earlier. He'd definitely been taken by surprise.

"And it gets worse," I went on, my eyes shifting to watch Melody's next reaction. "He killed a man that night."

"You can tell him the whole story, Jake," Melody said, a gentle smile on her face for me.

"There's more?" Mitch asked. "Wait, when did you say this happened?"

"Months ago," I said. "Mel, am I right with my guess? Something like six months now?"

"Yes," she said. "Almost six and a half."

"Wait," Mitch said. "You two have been a thing for *that* long? So Dad's been in a coma for half a year, and I'm only hearing about this *now?* What the hell, man? Just because I don't live there doesn't mean I'm not part of the family."

"No, we haven't been together that long," Melody

said. "Jake and I met because of that accident though."

"That's the rest of this particular secret," I said. "Dad didn't kill just anyone—he killed Melody's husband, Dan, who was also Liam's father."

"Jake, you moved in on the widow of the man our father killed?" Mitch said, censure wrapping his words in a tight fist. "Seriously, bro?"

At his cutting words, my mouth fell open in shock.

Chapter 45

No Holding Back

"MY HUSBAND WAS abusive," Melody said, jumping in to stem the rapidly escalating tension by turning the focus on herself. "So I wasn't exactly in traditional mourning."

"You don't have to explain it," I said. "Mitch, we're not doing anything wrong, so dial back the judgment, man."

"Okay, okay. I'm sorry," he replied, and I could tell that he meant it. "I'm just a little off kilter here. Feels like my family's edged me right out of the circle of trust. Can't imagine why you never thought it might be important to tell me any of this."

"You don't exactly make it easy," I told him—because it had to be said—feeling my resentments bubbling to the surface now. "And you do the same thing anyway. It's not like we know much about your life, either."

"M-Mitch," Max said. "J-Jake didn't tell you, it's t-true, but he d-didn't tell me or anyone else, either. Th-that's the other part of this. J-Jake just got r-released from the h-hospital. His b-blood pressure got so high that he p-passed out in his t-truck."

"Are you *serious?!* You didn't think I'd want to know my own twin was in the hospital? I can't believe any of you right now."

"Wow," Claire whispered again, surely still unaware of how clearly Lily's mic was picking up her voice.

"Bootleg Jake is the bizarro version. He's all the Jake, plus all the rage."

"Claire-bear, shh," Lily whispered. "No more truth bombs."

"J-Jake has to lower his s-stress levels, or this c-could happen again," Max went on, anger lacing each word as he ignored Claire's observation. She'd nailed it though—Mitch always carried a ready supply of unbridled rage inside of him. I was the laidback one by comparison, although that seemed ironic now, given that I'd almost killed myself via boiling stress. "S-so knock it off, M-Mitch. J-Jake has been carrying around this b-burden for months s-simply to protect us."

"No, Max, he's right," I said. "I'm sorry. It was a huge mistake, obviously. I about killed myself holding it in. I should have told you guys when it first happened. I know I should have. But I was so excited about Max's progress and the way things were unfolding for him with Lily. I didn't want to stop his forward momentum by clogging up his brain with more crap about Dad."

"Okay," Mitch said, his anger receding somewhat but clearly not dissipating entirely. "That explains why you didn't tell Max. But why didn't you tell *me?* Unless something else changed that I don't know about, we're still twins, man. You had to know I'd be here for you."

"I didn't...." I started, then glanced back at Melody's beautiful face. Just seeing her sitting there and loving me helped me drop a truth bomb of my own. "Honestly, I got so used to handling everything alone that, in a way, it never even *occurred* to me to tell you. As with all of Max's struggles through the years, I was simply on my own. I didn't think you'd care or come help me shoulder it all. You never have before, right? So maybe I figured if I didn't tell you this time, you couldn't let me down again."

Mitch sat back then, stunned, as hurt poured off him in waves.

"I can't believe you just said that," he finally replied.

"Yeah, well, it turns out that there's a lot of stuff I've been avoiding dealing with by shoving it down inside of me," I said. "And yeah, Max didn't oversell it—it almost killed me. But I'm trying to do things the right way now. No more secrets or holding back or doing everything by myself in the name of protecting everyone around me. That's why I arranged this call. I wanted to finally get everything out on the table. So why don't you do the same thing? What's the secret about Dad that *you're* hiding?"

"I told you," he said. "It's nothing. I misspoke."

"Not sure I believe you," I said.

"Good, because I can't believe you right now, either," he replied. "So, is there anything else we haven't covered yet?"

"J-Jake's gallbladder p-practically had to explode before he'd go s-see a doctor about it," Max added, shrugging when I shot him a look of irritation.

"What?!" Mitch yelled.

"It's not a big deal," I said. "Once they got my blood pressure down, they took out my gallbladder, too. Must have been running a two-for-one deal that day."

"Great," Mitch said, his anger eerily vanishing as quickly as it had appeared, the look on his face now vacant. "I'm glad you got it taken care of finally. Unless there's something more you guys need to unload on me, I've got to go."

"N-no," Max said after an awkward beat of silence passed. I couldn't bring myself to say anything more to him anyway, because he was responding exactly the way I was afraid he would. "Th-that's it."

"Nice to meet you, Melody," he said. "And good to see you again, Lily. But...yeah, I've got to go."

And without waiting for any replies, he disconnected from the call, his face disappearing from the screen.

*   *   *

"That went well," Claire whispered into the shocked silence.

"J-Jake, I'm s-so sorry," Max said.

"Not your fault," I assured him, the old familiar worries twisting inside my chest.

"I'm coming over," Melody announced, a look of alarm on her beautiful face. "Jake, do you hear me? I'll be there in a minute."

I nodded mutely, waving as the others disconnected from the call until I was alone again, staring into my own face on the screen.

How had things with Mitch gotten this far off track? And what secret was he harboring? It was definitely something, and I didn't believe for a minute that he'd simply misspoken earlier. Maybe I wasn't the only brother in our family who liked to hold things inside.

When Liam and Melody arrived, she walked right into my arms and held me tight—exactly what I needed most at that moment.

"I'm so sorry, honey," she said. "I know that wasn't how you wanted that conversation to go."

"I messed up," I told her. "Our family fractured a long time ago, of course, but I always thought that Max, Mitch, and I were on the same side. I thought we were a team. But now it's like there's this new fault line running through us. I thought that Dad was the only villain of the tale. Well, and Mom, too, because of her complete inaction. Now I think *I'm* the one who messed up. I was trying to be the glue that held us all together, but it turns out I'm more like poison than glue."

"Listen to me," she said, her tone fierce as she pulled back to look into my eyes. "There are lots of mistakes to go around in every family dynamic. Very rarely is one person totally to blame. And that goes for Dan and me, too, by the way. I sat back and let a lot of bad stuff happen in the name of peacekeeping. That's where *your* heart was—you were trying to keep the peace. But it seems like Mitch made mistakes of his own. He's apparently got a secret he's keeping from you guys, plus it's not like he ever made much of an effort to learn what was new with you two, right? So don't go down your old paths of internalizing this. Talk to me. Let it out. And just give Mitch some time to process things. He might surprise you yet."

"I hope you're right," I said. "I hope he forgives me. But what I really hope is that he comes back here, or at least visits once in a while. Without him, no matter how happy I am with you and Liam and Max as my family, I'm just not whole."

"I know, baby. I know."

She pulled from my embrace, grabbed my hand, and gently tugged me to the couch where Liam had flopped down. I sat and pulled them both into my arms as peace and comfort flooded through me. Yes, I had problems with Mitch. And yes, the situation with Dad was still right there, needing to be addressed.

But these two other, very precious people in my arms were my family, too, and they had to be my focus right now. I hugged them both as I said a silent prayer of thanks. Despite all the problems and hurdles we'd been forced to overcome, we ended up together, in each other's arms—which is right where we all belonged. We were a family, and this time I'd make sure no stress cracks or fault lines appeared.

"I love you both so much," I said, the feelings overwhelming me and causing my voice to crack.

"I love my mom, and I love you, too, Jake," Liam chimed in, joining in on the lovefest as he pulled back and smiled at me. I turned in shock to look at Melody, but she just smiled too and nodded.

"Yep, get used to it, Jake," she said. "We both love you, and we're always going to be right here for you, no matter what bad times might lie ahead. After what we've already overcome together? C'mon, you have to know it's true."

And I did. *Of course* she was right. Between the three of us, we'd been through a firestorm already. After all, it wasn't too long ago that I was sitting in my truck, weary and burdened, wondering if I could ever take a moment for myself. Liam had been locked in silence and trauma, and Melody had been isolated and alone. So yeah, we'd come far in a very short time, and a lot had changed for us. And anything the future might have in store was just going to have to be put on notice that the three of us were unstoppable. Together, we could face absolutely anything.

Contentment flowed through me then as I held onto them even more tightly, and a conviction of the very best kind wove itself through my heart and soul— the conviction that nothing again would ever divide us.

Thank You!

THANK YOU for reading Jake and Melody's story! I would appreciate it so much if you took a moment to rate or review it on your favorite site.

There's more Jake and Melody—as well as more Max and Lily—to come, as this is book two in the trilogy about the Cruz brothers. If you can't wait, Mitch's story is live now on Kindle Vella, but will be coming soon in ebook and paperback.

Sneak Peek!

Here's an advance look at Mitch's story, *What Separates Us: An Enemies-to-Lovers Romance*. Mitch has been separated from his family for years. Did he take off simply to escape the family drama—or was there more to it? What secret is he keeping about their father and, now that both Max and Jake have found love and happiness, will Mitch's loneliness become more than he can bear?

CHAPTER ONE

"OH MITCH," she giggled, digging her perfectly polished nails into my thigh, "you're so funny!"

"No one's ever said that to me in my life," I said, tossing back a slow mouthful of beer as I assessed her before swallowing and adding, "I'm not exactly known as a comedian."

"Well, that's crazy because you literally are!" she said again, her hand still clutching my leg in a maniacally tight squeeze. "You make me laugh literally all the time!"

I rolled my eyes; I couldn't even help the automatic response. And yeah, I know it was a jerk thing to do, but I think it was her constant and incorrect use of the word *literal* that had started poking holes in my attraction to her. Pick a new word. Please, for the love of God, buy a thesaurus.

Once I started noticing that, then my brain started

picking out every other little annoyance about her too and highlighting it for me. Constantly. Trust me, it was getting old, but as the stack of irritations grew, so did my unhappiness, both with her and with my whole life. I know it's stupidly inconsequential. Of course I realize how ridiculous and baseless my building resentments were against Tifanee—yes, that's how she spells it, and yeah, okay, that's one of the many things I don't like about her. Sue me.

I get it, I do. I understand that I'm not exactly coming off like a nice guy here, but then again, I guess I'm really *not* a nice guy. But I know that I used to be. And I think I'm still capable of it sometimes; I was nice to my baby brother and his new girlfriend, and I helped them out not long ago. So see? I'm not a total lost cause.

But what I am is weary. And angry. And lonely. And I was tired of being all of those things, but there I sat, with beautiful Tifanee and her stupid compliments driving a jackhammer through my last nerve.

"Mitchy, we've been together for six months now," she said as my brain tossed another item onto the stack. That "Mitchy" thing was just…what was I even doing with her? Every word out of her mouth created a dissonance in my head, and that had been true for a while. I don't know why she wasn't right for me. We'd met on a shoot—we're both models. We'd produced enough chemistry together to make some really killer shots that day, and I guess I thought that meant something. I think I saw that chemistry, mixed it together with the attraction, and saw it as a possible lifeline. Something to hold onto when the rage builds inside me. When the loneliness claws its way through my chest.

But I guess chemistry isn't the same thing as compatibility. Attraction sure isn't love. She was beautiful; of course she was. And I think she's smarter than I gave her credit for, because the more I started to pull back from her, the tighter she tried to hold on. Her holding on to me with both hands ended up displaying itself as a whole lot of fawning. She was constantly showering me with compliments, earned or not. That's why the "you're so funny" thing grated on me, rather than just wafting into the air between us—like any other harmless comment should—and floating away, unremarked upon and forgotten.

But I didn't want to just forget it and let it go. I was literally sick of her—yes, I know what I just did there—and I desperately needed to end the relationship. As lonely as I was, I didn't want *that*. I didn't want her. When you're with someone for months and still feel utterly alone, it's a pretty big hint that things aren't right.

"Mitchy?" she asked. "Did you hear me? We've been together for so long. I think it's time we moved in together. Why are we wasting money on two apartments? It's literally crazy when we could just be together all the time."

"I heard you," I said, as a vision of waking up and looking at her face across the top of my morning coffee every single day for the rest of my life drove a shudder of repulsion through me. I actually, physically shuddered, which definitely wasn't the reaction she was looking for, I'm sure. "Sorry, Tif, that's not what I want."

"But why drag out the inevitable?" she asked, not bothering to hide the hurt on her face. "What are we waiting for?"

"Honestly, I was waiting for this to feel right," I said, reaching down to peel her hand off my thigh. "But it doesn't feel right. And it never will."

"Are you…wait, are you *breaking up* with me?" she asked, tears forming in her eyes now. "No, I'm sorry! I didn't mean to push you. We don't have to move in together! Of course we don't. It was just an idea!"

"No, this isn't about that," I said, struggling to soften my words. "You didn't do anything wrong. You're a great person, and there's a man out there who will appreciate you. But that man can't be me."

"Why not?!" she said, tears turning to anger now. "Why can't it be you? We're great together."

"I'm not happy," I said with a shrug. "I haven't been for a really, really long time. And I don't just mean with you. I'm not happy in any part of my life. Something happened recently that really drove that home for me. I'm not happy with me, so I don't have anything inside me to offer to you."

"Whatever it is, we can get through it together, though," she said. "You don't open up to me. That's the problem. You literally never talk to me. I didn't know something happened recently, but if you'd just share it with me, I can help you get through it."

"I appreciate that, I do," I said. "But doesn't the fact that it never even occurred to me to talk to you about this tell you anything?"

"Why are you doing this?" she said, sitting back now. "Why are you pulling away from me when you need me the most?"

"That's the thing, Tif," I said. "Even when we're together, I'm still alone. And I don't see that changing anytime soon."

"That was a mean thing to say," she said, grabbing

her purse with a haughty sniff. "I don't need this. I can have any man I want. And you're kind of a jerk, did you know that?"

"Sorry," I said, pulling some cash out of my wallet and throwing it on the table before standing up. "But you're right. I'm just not a very nice guy."

I thought ending things with her would help me somehow, or maybe it would lift a little of the darkness from my soul. But as I walked into my quiet apartment that night and crawled into bed, I realized that all I felt was the sting of that old, familiar loneliness that had somehow become my only companion.

Acknowledgments

I HADN'T GOTTEN very far into Max's story, which I'd originally envisioned as a standalone book only, before it became very obvious to me that Jake needed a story of his own. After all, he surely had to have developed a savior complex after all those years of dedicating his life to his brother. His conflict seemed very clear and obvious to me, as did the journey he'd need to take to find his own happily-ever-after.

But that's when the story got tricky for me. I toyed with making his love interest be someone from the gym, but you could fit my knowledge about personal training into a thimble. So…maybe not! Eventually the idea of giving him yet another troubled boy to focus his energy on arose in my mind, and from there the idea for Melody was born.

I hope you enjoyed Jake and Melody's story, and I'd love to hear your thoughts about it in reviews, on social media, or via email! And don't forget to read Mitch's story, which will be out soon!

As always, I'm sending out all my love and thanks to my family and friends for all their support. And a huge thank you to my friend and editor Wil Mara, who manages to find time to help me, even in the middle of his own hectic schedule. You're the best!

About the Author

ANNE TROWBRIDGE loves writing romances that hit major emotional beats in swoony, angsty stories in which the couples really earn their happily ever afters. Expect banter, angst, and deeply emotional connections that resonate!

She lives in New Jersey with her husband, two kids, and two dogs. When she's not reading or writing, she's teaching language arts to middle schoolers, which really should involve medals for bravery. She grew up all over the Midwest and somehow still loves to travel and see new places.

Join her and learn more about upcoming books at:

https://www.annetrowbridgebooks.com/

https://linktr.ee/annetrowbridgebooks